The Christmas Genie

OTHER BOOKS BY DAN GUTMAN

....

The Talent Show

The Homework Machine

Return of the Homework Machine

Nightmare at the Book Fair

Getting Air

The CHRISTMAS Genie

DAN GUTMAN
AUTHOR OF: The HOMEWORK MACHINE

Illustrated by DAN SANTAT

SIMON & SCHUSTER BOOKS FOR YOUNG READERS
New York   London   Toronto   Sydney

SIMON & SCHUSTER BOOKS FOR YOUNG READERS
An imprint of Simon & Schuster Children's Publishing Division
1230 Avenue of the Americas, New York, New York 10020

This book is a work of fiction. Any references to historical events, real people, or real locales are used fictiously. Other names, characters, places, and incidents are products of the author's imagination, and any resemblance to actual events or locales or persons, living or dead, is entirely coincidental.

SIMON & SCHUSTER BOOKS FOR YOUNG READERS is a trademark of Simon & Schuster, Inc.
For information about special discounts for bulk purchases, please contact Simon & Schuster Special Sales at 1-866-506-1949 or business@simonandschuster.com.
The Simon & Schuster Speakers Bureau can bring authors to your live event. For more information or to book an event, contact the Simon & Schuster Speakers Bureau at 1-866-248-3049 or visit our website at www.simonspeakers.com.
Also available in a Simon & Schuster Books for Young Readers hardcover edition.
Book design by Tom Daly
The text for this book is set in Horley Old Style MT.
The illustrations for this book are rendered digitally.
Manufactured in the United States of America • 0811 OFF
First Simon & Schuster Books for Young Readers paperback edition October 2010
4 6 8 10 9 7 5
The Library of Congress has cataloged the hardcover edition as follows:
Gutman, Dan.
The Christmas genie/Dan Gutman; illustrated by Dan Santat—1st ed.
p. cm.
Summary: When a meteorite crashes into a fifth-grade classroom at Lincoln School in Oak Park, Illinois, the genie inside agrees to grant the class a Christmas wish—if they can agree on one within an hour.
ISBN 978-1-4169-9001-7 (hc)
[1. Genies—Fiction. 2. Wishes—Fiction. 3. Schools—Fiction. 4. Christmas—Fiction. 5. Meteorites—Fiction.]
Title.
PZ7.G9846Chr2009
[Fic]—dc22
200917765
ISBN 978-1-4169-9002-4 (pbk)
ISBN 978-1-4391-5826-5 (eBook)

To my editor, Emily Meehan,
who always pushes me to be better

Acknowledgments

Thanks to Liza Voges, Nathan Katz, Deb Licorish,
Laurie Bushey, Nina Wallace, Janet Goodman,
Theresa Wolfe, Jane Babcock, and all the kids
who shared their deepest, darkest wishes.

The Christmas Genie

PART ONE Before

MRS. WALTERS'S CLASS

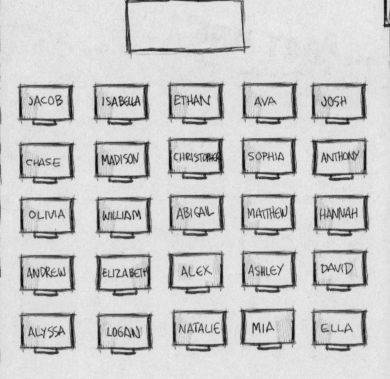

JACOB	ISABELLA	ETHAN	AVA	JOSH
CHASE	MADISON	CHRISTOPHER	SOPHIA	ANTHONY
OLIVIA	WILLIAM	ABIGAIL	MATTHEW	HANNAH
ANDREW	ELIZABETH	ALEX	ASHLEY	DAVID
ALYSSA	LOGAN	NATALIE	MIA	ELLA

That Thing That Happened

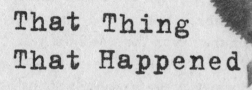

You're probably not going to believe this story. Fine. That's okay. It's a free country. You can believe what you want to believe. Or not. But I know what happened. Because I was *there*.

Where is "there"? Lincoln School in Oak Park, Illinois. Fifth grade. This is what my class looks like.

Well, that's what my class would look like if you were hanging from the ceiling like Michelangelo and drawing a picture of it. But I have no idea why you would want to do a crazy thing like that.

That's me, in the second row on the left side, by the window. My name is Chase. My best friend is Alex. He's on my basketball team, but we're not allowed to sit next to each other because he's always cracking jokes and distracting me. So we had to be "separated."

It's a pretty good group of kids, I guess. Well, except for Abigail, who thinks she's so great just because she's got a cool cell phone; Mia, the wet blanket; Logan, who threw my umbrella up on the roof of the school last year; and Christopher, who is just plain dumb as a box of rocks. Everybody else is relatively normal. Our teacher, Mrs. Walters, always says we're the "chattiest" group she ever had. I don't think that means we're brilliant conversationalists. It just means we talk too much.

That's her, in the front of the room. One time I saw Mrs. Walters at the supermarket and I kind of freaked out because it was like, *What is my teacher doing in a supermarket?*

Okay, enough setup. None of that stuff is important, anyway. The important thing to know is that if you look at the picture, that's where we all were when this thing happened that you may or may not believe. Like I said, I don't care one way or another.

It happened just before winter vacation, on December 21. That's the winter solstice, and in case you don't know what that means, it's the first day of winter and the shortest day of the year. It has something to do with the distance and angle of the sun. I'm kind of into science stuff. Anyway, everybody was excited about Christmas, Hanukkah, Kwanzaa or whatever holiday it is that they celebrate. Nobody was really focusing too much on what Mrs. Walters was saying. We were all thinking about the presents we were going to get, the ski trips we were going to go on, and the family reunions we were going to have as soon as school let out. You know, all the holiday stuff. It's a nice time of year. Mrs. Walters put cheery decorations all over the walls of the class. Everybody was feeling good.

I do remember this much—when it happened, Mrs. Walters was talking about meteorites. She's an astronomy nut, and at night she's taking graduate classes because she's working on her Ph.D. in astrophysics. She tries to bring astronomy into everything she teaches us. Like, we'll be doing math and she'll have us adding, subtracting, multiplying, and dividing stars or planets instead of apples and oranges. Or we'll be doing health and she'll start talking about whether or not germs can survive in outer space without oxygen. I feel sorry for Mrs. Walters's family because they have to hear this stuff *all* the time.

Meteorites are kind of cool. You may not realize this, but there's a whole lot of stuff flying around in outer space, and it all has different names. Like, meteorites are rocks from space that hit the Earth, but meteors are still in space. Comets, meteoroids, and asteroids all orbit the sun. But meteoroids are small, asteroids are bigger, and comets have a tail. I know all this stuff because Mrs. Walters talks about it all the time.

"One day in 1998," Mrs. Walters told us, almost in a whisper, "some boys were playing basketball in a driveway in Monahans, Texas. And suddenly, they looked up and saw a meteorite come flying out of the sky! It crashed into the vacant lot next door to them. Can you imagine that? It was all over the papers and the TV news."

"That must have been cool," said David, who thinks everything is cool, even stuff that is totally uncool.

"You mean I might be outside minding my own business and a giant rock could come flying out of the sky?" asked Ashley. "That would be terrifying!"

6

Ashley is the kind of kid who worries about every dumb thing that could possibly happen to her. Like, what are the chances that anybody would ever get hit by a meteorite?

"Did the meteorite ruin the basketball game?" asked Jacob, who sits in front of me. I like sports too, but Jacob is obsessed. All that guy ever talks about is sports.

"I would think so!" said Mrs. Walters.

We were having this discussion when suddenly there was this loud *BOOM . . . BOOM . . . BOOM* outside.

I guess it could have been a sonic boom. That's the noise that an object makes when it travels faster than the speed of sound—about 750 miles per hour—at sea level. I looked it up in one of my science books. But it wasn't a plane. The sound was really close, like it was right outside. We all turned to look out the window. And then, maybe a second or two later, there was a *crash* and the window next to me just *exploded*! Glass was flying all over the place. Whatever it was that smashed through the window was heading straight for my desk.

Everything happened so fast after that, there wasn't a lot of time to react.

Somehow, I had the sense to cover my eyes with one arm and dive off my chair. I hit the floor next to Madison, who sits next to me. There was a lot of shouting and screaming. I didn't see anything after that.

When I finally looked up, my desk was shattered. I mean *shattered*. There was something half-buried in the floor underneath it. It looked like a rock, and it was about the size of a small garbage can. If I hadn't dived out of the way, it would have crushed my legs, or maybe gone right through me.

I would have been dead.

The Amazing Part

It was amazing! But that's not even the *really* amazing part of the story. I'll get to the really amazing part in a minute.

Naturally, everybody freaked out, even the cool kids who like to pretend nothing bothers them. We were all on the floor, hiding under our desks and covering our heads. The girls were screaming. Somebody was crying. I figured it must have been a bomb. Maybe our school was being attacked by terrorists.

"What was *that*?" asked Ella, who sits in the back row.

"Remain calm!" Mrs. Walters shouted, with panic in her voice. "Everybody stay under your desk!"

Like staying under a desk was going to protect us from a bomb, right? I didn't have a desk to stay under anyway, because my desk was in a million pieces. I just lay there on the floor, dazed.

About a minute passed before anybody said anything.

"Is everybody okay?" asked Mrs. Walters.

We got up slowly. All of my body parts seemed to be intact. No blood anywhere. I was afraid another bomb might come flying through the window, and thought we should just get out of there. But nobody was making a move for the door.

"I think there's a piece of glass in my arm," Ashley groaned. She sounded like she was going to cry.

Mrs. Walters went to help Ashley, while the rest of us gathered around the thing that was stuck in the floor. There was smoke pouring out of it.

"What do you think it is?" asked Olivia.

"I'll tell you what it is," said Ava, the walking encyclopedia. "It's a meteor."

"It can't be a meteor," I told her. "Meteors don't hit the Earth. It's a meteor*ite*."

Everybody seemed to be okay. There wasn't even any glass in Ashley's arm. The big crybaby

just hit it against something while she was diving under her desk.

"It *is* a meteorite!" Mrs. Walters exclaimed as she got down on her hands and knees to look at it. Her eyes were wide with excitement.

That's when our principal, Mr. Hamilton, charged in the door. Mrs. Walters jumped up and stood in front of the meteorite so Mr. Hamilton couldn't see it.

"I heard a crash," Mr. Hamilton said. "Is everyone all right?"

Mr. Hamilton has to deal with lots of crisis situations all the time. Like, every year there's always some dope who pulls the fire alarm for no reason. Or that time we were in fourth grade and Miss Rassky found a snake in the cloakroom. *That* was interesting! But I'm pretty sure this was the first time a meteorite had ever come flying into a classroom.

"A desk broke," Mrs. Walters said, lamely.

Mr. Hamilton looked around suspiciously. "I'll get the custodian," he said. And he left.

Once it was clear that everybody was okay, we weren't afraid anymore. We were all excited about what had happened.

"I can't believe a rock fell out of the sky and landed right here in our class!" said Alyssa. "What are the odds of that happening?"

"Well, it had to land *somewhere*," Ella pointed out. "The odds are just as good that it would land here as they are that it would land anywhere else."

Ella is so sensible. Sensible can be annoying.

"But it landed here just as we were talking about meteorites!" I pointed out.

"This is the most exciting thing that ever happened to me!" Mrs. Walters said with wonder as we gathered around the hole in the floor. "I've been waiting my whole life to get my hands on a meteorite. I'll be able to study this and write it up as a research project."

I wanted to touch it, but common sense told me that when something is smoking, it's hot. And hot stuff burns your skin. And burning skin hurts. That didn't stop William, who is on our school football team and looks like he's in eighth grade. He's really good at football, but he needs a common sense transplant. William put his finger on the meteorite and immediately pulled it away.

"Owwwwwwwww!" he said, shaking his hand.

"I didn't mean I was going to get my hands on it right away, William," Mrs. Walters scolded.

I leaned closer. It didn't look like a regular rock. It wasn't smooth. Mrs. Walters got a magnifying glass from her desk and held it up to the meteorite. There were small pits in it. Abigail took out her stupid cell phone camera and shot some pictures.

"This could be four and a half *billion* years old," Mrs. Walters told us. "It may provide clues to the solar nebula, the swirling cloud of gas and dust that gave rise to the sun and the planets. If it contains water, that would suggest it had an encounter with a comet, which is essentially a cosmic snowball."

"Cosmic Snowball would be a good name for a rock band," said Logan. What a dope.

"What do you think it's made of?" asked Josh. "Lava?"

Mrs. Walters went over to the whiteboard and took one of the magnetic clips she uses to hold up papers and stuff. She touched it against the meteorite and it stuck with a click.

"It's made of iron," said Ava, who knows everything.

"Just think," Natalie said, "this thing could have been flying around space for centuries. For *eternity*. Maybe it's been to the edge of the universe and back."

"There are no edges to the universe," Ava said. "The universe just goes on forever."

"How do *you* know?" said Ella. "The universe can't go on forever. It has to end *some*where."

"And what do you think happens after that point?" asked Mrs. Walters.

"Nobody knows," Josh said.

"God knows," said Ava.

"What should we do with it, Mrs. Walters?" asked Ella. "Should we call the police?"

"No!" Mrs. Walters exclaimed.

"What would the police do?" asked Ethan. "Maybe we should call the science museum. They would know what to do."

"No!" Mrs. Walters exclaimed.

"I say we call the news," said Andrew. "I'll bet they'd send a camera crew over here. We'll become famous like those kids in Texas. Hey, I bet we could make some money out of this thing." Andrew is always talking about getting famous and making lots of money.

"No!" Mrs. Walters exclaimed. "Don't call *anybody*! I want to be the first to study it. This will be our little secret, okay?"

"Okay," we all agreed.

The smoke had stopped coming out of the meteorite. Mrs. Walters leaned over and touched a piece of paper against it. The paper didn't burn or turn black. Then she tapped a finger against it for a moment.

"It's cooling off," she told us. "You can touch it gently if you want."

We all leaned over to touch the meteorite except for Ashley, who said she was afraid— of course. It felt warm, but not too hot to hold your hand against it. There were twenty-four of us reaching out to touch it at the same time. I rubbed a finger against it, and so did some of the other kids. Nothing came off on my skin. It didn't burn.

Let me just warn you that this is when the *really* amazing part happened.

While we were rubbing our hands against the meteorite, it started to vibrate slightly and give off a humming sound. Then it started to glow yellowish red. It was like there was some kind of energy source coming from deep within it. There was the crackle of sparks. We all pulled our hands off and backed away. Something very strange was happening.

And then . . . this *thing* started to rise up out of the meteorite.

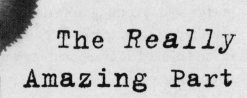

The *Really* Amazing Part

Okay, this is the part of the story that you might find a little bit hard to believe. But as I said, I was there when it happened and you weren't. So who are you gonna believe, your own sense of what's possible, or me?

The thing that rose out of the meteorite looked human, with regular facial features and long hair tied back in a ponytail. It was a little *man*! Like a genie. But he wasn't wearing a turban. In fact, he was wearing a tie-dyed shirt and flip-flops.

When the smoke cleared, I could see he was about three feet tall, and he floated a few feet above the meteorite like a balloon. It was sort of a Princess Leia/holographic/avatar kind of thing. His eyes were closed, but when everybody started screaming and freaking out, he opened them. Mrs. Walters said a curse word that I'm sure

you've heard a million times, but never out of the mouth of a *teacher*. We all backed away from the meteorite. Abigail was trembling as she fumbled with her cell phone camera. Mrs. Walters just stared at the little man, her mouth open.

"What *is* it?" asked Josh.

"Maybe it's a genie," said Isabella.

"Don't be silly," Ella said. "There's no such thing as genies."

"He's kinda cute," said Abigail.

William, who you would think would have learned not to touch stuff, went to poke the genie with his finger.

"Hey!" the genie suddenly shouted. "Getcher filthy paws off me!"

We all jumped back. A few kids fell down.

"You . . . speak?" Mrs. Walters croaked. "English?"

"Any dope can speak English," the genie said. "It's Japanese that's tricky."

Abigail took a picture of the genie with her cell phone camera.

"Make sure ya get my good side," he said, posing. And then, he let out a loud, nasty burp. It lasted about five seconds.

"Man," the genie said when the burp was finally done, "I been holding that baby in for thirteen million light years."

"You *are* a genie, aren't you?" I asked.

"Well, I ain't Santa Claus, buster, that's for sure," the genie said. "Lock the door."

Nobody moved. We couldn't stop staring at him.

"I said lock the door, you dimwits!" the genie shouted. "What does a guy haveta do to get some cooperation around this joint?"

Mrs. Walters jumped up and locked the door. She did it just in time, too. Because as soon as the door clicked we heard the voice of Mr. Wilson, our school custodian.

"Is everything okay in there?" hollered Mr. Wilson through the door.

Mrs. Walters put a finger to her lips and told us all to *shhhhhhhhh*.

"Yes, everything's fine, Mr. Wilson!" she yelled. "Just a little accident with a desk. You can clean it up later."

Everybody turned and looked at the genie again.

"Now listen up and listen good," he told us.

"What I'm gonna say is private. Nobody breathes a word of this to anybody, you got it?"

"Got it," we all said.

"You too, teach," said the genie.

"I won't tell a soul," whispered Mrs. Walters.

"Okay, here's the deal," the genie continued. "Ya ever been on a really long car drive? You get a little cranky, right? Well, I been traveling through space for a *long* time. But because you brats were lucky enough to be in the right place at the right time, I'm gonna grant you a wish. It's just my little way of saying thanks for freeing me from the meteorite. Think of it as a Christmas present from me."

"He's a *Christmas* genie!" gushed Madison.

"Whatever," muttered the genie.

"Do you have a name?" asked Josh.

"It don't matter what my name is," said the genie.

"C'mon, what's the big deal?" asked Alex. "Tell us your name."

"I'll bet he has a funny name," said Jacob. "That's why he doesn't want to tell us."

"It is *not* a funny name," said the genie. "It's a perfectly normal name."

"Then tell us what it is," Ava said.

"Yeah," we all said.

"Okay, okay, I'll tell ya," the genie said. "But then we get on with it. Deal?"

"Deal!" we all agreed.

"My name is Bob," said the genie.

Everybody cracked up.

"Well, it *is* normal," Ella said.

"Bob?" asked Ethan. "Are you kidding?"

"Who names a genie 'Bob'?" asked Alex. "A genie should have a cool name like Alazar, or Hippocampus."

"That's a part of the *brain*, you dork," said Ava.

"Look, my name is Bob," said the genie. "Deal with it. I can leave, y'know. Maybe the class next door wants to have *their* wish come true."

"No!" everybody started yelling. "Don't leave! We'll take it! We'll take the wish."

"That's more like it," said Bob the genie.

"One wish?" said Logan. "You're supposed to grant *three* wishes. "In *Aladdin*, the genie granted three wishes."

"Well, this ain't *Aladdin*, smart guy," Bob told Logan. Then he blew his nose into his sleeve.

"I find it extremely difficult to believe that

this . . . apparition . . . is actually a genie," said Mrs. Walters. "Granting wishes is just a fantasy. Scientifically, it's impossible."

"Yeah," said Josh. "This could be some special effect. Like in the movies. Or maybe we're hallucinating."

"If you're really a genie, do something miraculous," I said.

"How about I turn one of you brats into a frog?" Bob suggested.

"That would be cool," said David.

About a second later, Genie Bob whirled around and pointed his finger at David, who disappeared in a puff of smoke. On the desk where David was sitting, there was a big cockroach. Everybody screamed.

"Where's David!?" yelled Mrs. Walters. "What did you do to him?"

"Kill it!" shouted Christopher. "There's a roach in the class!"

"No! Don't!" yelled Ella. "Genie Bob turned David into a cockroach! Oh man, his mom is gonna be upset!"

"I thought you said you were going to turn him into a frog," said Alyssa.

"I changed my mind," said Genie Bob. "I'm in a bad mood today."

"You change that cockroach back into a boy this very minute!" scolded Mrs. Walters.

"Okay, okay," Genie Bob said. "Sheesh. Lighten up, teach."

A second later, the cockroach disappeared in a puff of smoke. Instead of the cockroach, on the desk where the cockroach had been sitting, was David.

"David!" Mrs. Walters shouted as she hugged him. "Are you all right?"

"That was *cool*!" David said.

"I guess you really *are* a Christmas genie," said Mrs. Walters.

"You're darn tootin', sister," said Genie Bob.

"So we get to make a wish?" Natalie asked. "Any wish we want?"

"*Si*," said Bob. "*Oui*. Affirmative. Yes."

"Well, here's my wish," Logan said. "I wish for a million wishes. Ha! So there!"

Genie Bob glared at Logan. I thought he might turn him into a cockroach too, or something even worse.

"Ya think you're pretty clever, eh, punk?"

Genie Bob said. "Ya think I never heard *that* one before? You think I just fell off the turnip truck, pal? Look, this ain't no negotiation. This ain't no game show. I make the rules around here. You get one wish and that's *it*. Take it or leave it."

"We'll take it!" we all shouted. "We'll take it!"

"Now you're showing some smarts," said Genie Bob. "Okay, here are the ground rules. Ya get a wish. Anything ya want. But here's the catch. I need your answer in one hour, because I can't hang around with you chumps all day. I got things to do."

"You've been trapped in a meteorite for thirteen million light years," Ella said. "What's your rush?"

"None of your beeswax," said Genie Bob. "I got people to see, places to go. I'll give you one hour. Think you can come up with a wish in an hour?"

"Sure!" we all said.

"Good," Genie Bob said. "Because if you don't, I'm gonna cancel your Christmas vacation."

"You can't do that!" Josh said.

"No?" Genie Bob asked. "I turned your friend here into a cockroach, didn't I? Canceling a vacation would be a piece of cake. So make it snappy. Choose it or lose it."

I looked over at the clock on the wall. It was 1:50. We had until just before dismissal to come up with a wish.

"We need to be fair about this," Mrs. Walters said, walking over to her desk. "I'm going to pass out an index card for every student in the class. Think it over and write down your wish. Then we'll look over all the wishes together and decide as a class which one makes the most sense. Does that sound fair to everyone?"

"Yes," we all agreed.

I'll tell you, Mrs. Walters can find a way to turn *anything* into an assignment.

As she walked around the room passing out index cards, I thought about my wish. If I could have anything in the world, what would I want? There are so many things I wish I had. It's hard to narrow it down to a single wish.

"Oh, one more thing," Bob said. "Remember the old saying—be careful what ya wish for."

And then he let out a weird, otherworldly laugh.

PART TWO During

This was a very important decision, maybe the most crucial decision we would make in our entire lives. I looked at my blank index card and started to put together a list in my head of all the things I wish I had. . . .

•A new video game system

•And a bunch of cool games to go with it, of course

•A snowboard

•A new bike (I left my old one out in the rain and it got all rusted.)

•A robot that would clean my room

•The Cubs winning the World Series . . .

This was going to be hard! There was so much stuff I wanted. How could I choose just one thing? But then I thought of the perfect wish, the wish that would make all the other wishes come true. I wrote it down. . . .

WISH #1:
I WISH I HAD ALL THE MONEY IN THE WORLD.

Nice wish, huh? If I had all the money in the world, I would live like a king. I could buy every video game that existed. I'd buy all the snowboards and bikes and robots I wanted. I'd buy the Cubs, and then I'd buy all the best players in the game so the Cubs would finally win the World Series. The people of Chicago would love me!

I'd buy my own private jet so I could go wherever I wanted and not have to wait at the airport and go through security and all that stuff. I'd buy a new house for my parents, because my brother and I have to share a bedroom which really stinks, especially when he snores.

It would be great to have all the money in the world. I couldn't imagine that anybody could come up with a better wish.

Mrs. Walters collected up all the index cards and put them in a big bowl. Hannah was the last one to turn in her card. She just kept writing and writing until everybody started yelling at her to hurry up. Finally she turned her card in. Mrs. Walters swished the cards all around with her hand, closed her eyes, and pulled one out of the bowl.

As it happened, it was *mine*! Mrs. Walters read it out loud to the class.

"That would be cool to have all the money in the world," David said.

"You could buy anything," said Abigail. "Anything you wanted."

"That's the idea," I said.

"Yeah, let's go with that one," Matthew said. "What's the point of wishing for anything else? We're ready."

"So that's your wish?" said Genie Bob. "That was fast. Ya sure ya don't wanna think it over a little?"

"Yup," I said. "That's what we want. All the money in the world."

"Is that your final answer?" asked Genie Bob.

"Wait!" said Mia from the back row. "Can I just say one thing? If you had all the money in the world, Chase, a lot of people would want to rob you. Did you think of that?"

"So what?" I said. "If I had all the money in the world, I could build an electric fence around my gigantic mansion. Anybody who tried to rob me would get the shock of their life."

Mia is a pain. No matter how good things are, she can always find some bad news. That's why Alex and I call her "the wet blanket" behind her back.

"You wouldn't be able to go out in public, you know," said Mia.

"Who needs to go out in public?" I said. "If I needed anything, I'd send my flunkies out to get it for me."

"So you would just stay home all the time, Chase?" asked Mrs. Walters.

"Sure, why not?" I said. "My house would have every video game and movie in the world. I'd have a cool game room, my own skate park, a food court, a swimming pool—"

"Even so, I think it would be boring to stay home all the time," Ashley said.

"You know, it just occurred to me that if one person had all the money in the world," said Natalie, "then nobody else in the world will have any money at *all*."

"Well, yeah," said Logan. "Duh!"

"But if nobody else had any money, you wouldn't be able to buy anything," Natalie said.

"Why not?" I asked.

"How could a store stay open if they didn't have any money?" asked Natalie. "They couldn't buy any stuff to sell to people. They'd have no inventory."

"Natalie makes a good point," said Mrs. Walters. "All the restaurants would have to close too, because they couldn't buy any food."

"And if you went into a store to buy something, they wouldn't be able to give you change," Natalie said, "because *you'd* have all the money in the world."

"If I had all the money in the world," I said, "why would I need change?"

"The point is, there would *be* no stores," said Mia. "No McDonald's. No Wal-Mart. No Staples. No malls. No nothing. They'd all go out of business."

"No Abercrombie & Fitch?" asked Abigail, visibly upset. "No Hollister? No Aéropostale? Where will I go to shop?"

"You couldn't shop," said Alyssa. "There would be no stores. Chase would have all the money. You'd have to make your own clothes."

"The whole economy would collapse," said Mia. "Your money would become worthless pieces of paper. We would have to go back to living off the land, the way people did thousands of years ago."

"I never thought of it that way," I admitted.

Maybe having all the money in the world wasn't such a great idea after all. Hmmm, this wasn't going to be as easy as I thought it would be.

"So you've changed your mind, Chase?" asked Mrs. Walters.

"I guess so," I said.

"Wait a minute!" Genie Bob said. "The kid

had a good wish. You should go with all the money in the world, so I can get out of here."

"You said we have an hour," Mrs. Walters said, "so be quiet!"

Bob made a *hmmph* noise and shot a mean look at Mrs. Walters.

"How about just wishing for a pot of gold buried in your backyard?" suggested Alex.

"Then you would have to dig it up," Ella said. "Why not just wish for a pot of gold in your living room?"

"Let's not be so hasty," Mrs. Walters said. "Let's see what the rest of you wished for."

"Fine," said Genie Bob, looking at the clock impatiently, "Sheesh, I bet Santa Claus doesn't have to put up with this aggravation."

Mrs. Walters pulled another index card out of the bowl.

WISH #2:

I WISH I HAD A MILLION DOLLARS.

"That was mine!" said Abigail, who sits in the middle of the room.

I couldn't believe Abigail wished for a million dollars. She lives in this huge house and her parents give her every stupid piece of jewelry and junk she wants. They must be millionaires ten times over already.

"Well, that seems a little more reasonable," Mrs. Walters said. "A million dollars is also a lot of money, but it would still leave a lot more money for the rest of the people in the world. To be honest, though, wishing for money seems a bit . . . shallow . . . to me."

"I'm shallow," William said quickly. "I wish I had a million dollars. Let's go with that."

"Great!" said Genie Bob, clapping his little genie hands together.

"What do you mean, let's go with that?" said Hannah. "It's not *your* decision, William! It's *our* decision. We should have a class vote before we decide on *anything*."

"That makes sense," Mrs. Walters said. "All those in favor of wishing for a million dollars, raise your hand."

About half the class raised their hands.

"And all those opposed, raise your hand."

The other half raised their hands.

"Wait a minute," Ella said. "If we wish for a million dollars, who gets the money?"

"I do, of course," said Abigail. "It was *my* wish."

"I just thought of something. The wish was

for *us*," Elizabeth said. "*All* of us. Isn't that right?"

"Ya get one wish," Genie Bob replied. "What ya do with it is your business."

"It's not fair if we wish for a million dollars and Abigail gets to keep it all," said Matthew.

"That's right," said Logan.

"What if we divided the million dollars equally between all of you?" Mrs. Walters suggested. "That would be fair, wouldn't it?"

I rushed to take out my calculator. So did everybody else. 1,000,000 . . . divided by 25 kids in the class . . . equals . . . 40,000.

"Forty grand?" I said, disappointed. "That can't be right."

"It's right," Isabella said. "I got the same answer."

"Forty thousand dollars doesn't seem like so much," Abigail said.

"What are you talking about?" said Anthony. "You can buy a lot of stuff with forty thousand bucks."

"You can't buy a house," Olivia said. "Isn't that right, Mrs. Walters? Houses cost a lot more than forty thousand dollars."

"That's true," Mrs. Walters said.

"My parents paid almost a *million* dollars for our house," Abigail bragged.

"None of us even *needs* a house," said Isabella. "We all have a place to live as it is."

"How about a car?" Christopher said. "Can you buy a car for forty thousand dollars?"

"Absolutely," Mrs. Walters said. "You can buy a very nice car."

"Can you buy a Lamborghini?" asked Christopher.

"I don't know," Mrs. Walters said. "I think that might cost a lot more."

"Then forget it," Christopher said. "That's the car I want. A Lamborghini Gallardo Spyder. That car rocks."

"We can't drive for, like, five years anyway," said Ella. "Why should we want a car?"

"Yeah, what's the point of wishing for something if you have to wait years to get it?" Olivia said.

"Because cars are cool," said David.

"I don't even like cars," said Hannah. "Cars cause global warming. Especially those sports cars and SUVs."

41

"Oh, here we go," said Logan. "Save-the-world time."

"We're not wishing for a car!" Abigail said. "We're wishing for a million dollars. Or forty thousand, anyway. You can buy whatever you want with your share."

"Hey, would we have to pay taxes on that money?" asked Ella.

"By law, I gotta report all wishes to the Internal Revenue Service," said Genie Bob. "So the answer to your question is yeah."

"How much taxes would we have to pay on a million bucks, Mrs. Walters?" asked Josh.

"Gee, I'm not sure," Mrs. Walters said. "Teachers don't make that kind of money! I would guess it would be around thirty-five percent."

I didn't have to take out my calculator. Thirty-five percent of a million is 350,000.

"What!?" said William. "Three hundred fifty thousand bucks in *taxes*? That's not fair!"

I took out my calculator again. If you take 350,000 away from 1,000,000, it leaves 650,000. And if you divide that by 25 kids in the class, it comes to 26,000.

"Hey," I told everybody, "our forty grand just turned into twenty-six grand."

"Forget it," Christopher said. "It's not worth it. Let's wish for something else."

"Yeah, something you don't have to pay taxes on," said Anthony.

Mrs. Walters pulled another index card out of the bowl.

WISH #3:

I WISH I HAD A TRUCK FULL OF CANDY.

"Now you're talkin' my language!" William jumped up and shouted. Mrs. Walters told him to sit down and be quiet.

"That one was mine," Matthew said. "Just think about it. A truck full of Kit Kats, 3 Musketeers, Twix, Hershey bars, Crunch, Tootsie Rolls—"

"That would be cool," said David.

"I don't particularly like chocolate," said Elizabeth.

"What?" Logan asked. "Are you brain-damaged? Everybody likes chocolate."

"Logan!" said Mrs. Walters.

"Well, I don't," said Elizabeth. "I try to eat healthy."

"If we had a truck full of candy," said Mia the wet blanket, "some of it might reach its expiration date before we had the chance to eat it."

"So we would eat it really fast," suggested Ethan. "Problem solved."

"If we ate it really fast we'd get sick," Mia said.

"And fat," said Elizabeth. "You know, obesity is a major problem in this country. Diabetes too."

"Candy rots your teeth," Alyssa added.

"Not if you brush frequently," Ella said.

"Maybe wishing for a truck full of candy

isn't the smartest idea," said Olivia.

"What is the problem with you people?" Matthew shouted. "Candy is the best thing in the world! What else would anyone want? I wish I had a magic candy machine that never ran out of candy, and you didn't even have to put money into it to get the candy out."

"Y'know, it's not like it's such a big deal getting candy," said Ella. "You can just go to any supermarket or 7-Eleven and get a candy bar for less than a dollar. I think we should wish for something that we *can't* get."

"Good point, Ella," Mrs. Walters said.

"You can't get a *truck full* of candy at a store," said Matthew.

"Where would you put it, anyway?" asked Ella.

"Put what?" asked Matthew.

"The *truck*," Ella said.

"Who cares where you'd put it?" Matthew asked.

"Well, you've got to put it *someplace*," Mia said. "You can't just leave a truck out on the street all the time. The police would give you a ticket."

What a party pooper that girl is.

"My dad would take the truck after we ate all the candy," said Matthew. "His truck is a piece of junk."

"What if *my* dad wants the truck?" asked Logan.

"What kind of a truck are we talking about?" asked William. "One of those little pickups? Or an eighteen-wheeler? We would have to specify the type of truck in the wish."

"You know," Mia said, "if a truck full of candy was parked anywhere, people would find out and steal the candy."

"We would lock the truck!" Matthew said, slapping his forehead. "Look, it doesn't even *have* to be a truck! That's just a *container* to hold the candy. I could have wished for a giant *bowl* full of candy."

"Then we would have to worry about what to do with the bowl when the candy was finished," Mia said.

"At least we can get some use out of a truck," said Madison. "You can't do *anything* with a giant bowl."

"Sure you can," Jacob said. "You can turn it into a swimming pool. Then we could go swimming."

"In that case, we might as well just wish for a swimming pool filled with candy to begin with," said Natalie.

"I don't like swimming," Ashley said. "I'm a terrible swimmer."

"And the first time it rains, our candy would be ruined," said Mia.

"Not if we covered the pool," Ella pointed out.

"We could cover it with a *truck!*" Alex suggested.

"I wish we had a swimming pool filled with root beer floats," Josh said, "and it never runs out of root beer no matter how much we drink. And the ice cream never melts."

At that point, everybody started yelling at one another. Genie Bob was rubbing his forehead like he had a headache.

"Man, Santa Claus has it easy," he muttered. "He just sits there and kids tell him what they want. What a life! Some people have it made."

"Hey, what is it with you and Santa Claus?" I asked. "What did Santa ever do to you?"

"What did he do to me?" Genie Bob said, sneering. "What did he to do me?"

"Yeah!" we all said.

"I'll tell you what he did to me," Genie Bob said. "He ruined my life! That's what he did to me!"

"How did Santa Claus ruin your life?" Elizabeth asked.

"You really want to know?"

"Yes!" we all shouted.

"Claus and I go way back," Genie Bob said. "I grew up at the North Pole. We went to school together. That guy is a jerk. When I was a kid, he used to beat me up and take my lunch money. Him and his boys."

"His boys?" I said. "You mean . . . the elves?"

"That's right," Bob said. "Those short guys he hangs out with. His posse."

"You let a bunch of elves beat you up?" asked Christopher. "That's pathetic, man!"

"Hey, those elves are tenacious," Bob said. "You've seen 'em work."

"Wait a minute," Ella said. "You're just making all this stuff up. Santa Claus doesn't even exist. Everybody knows that."

"Doesn't exist, eh?" said Genie Bob as he lifted up his little shirt. "You see that scar?

That's where Rudolph the Red-Nosed Reindeer bit me! Claus told him to do it. I *hate* that guy! And look what happened. Claus grows up to be one of the most famous men in history, this jolly guy who brings joy and happiness to millions of people all over the world. Do you know what I'm famous for?"

"What?" we all said.

"You got a computer in this class?" Genie Bob asked. "Go to Google and do a search for the word 'genie.' See what pops up first."

We all gathered around the computer at the back of the class. Ava went to Google and typed in GENIE. We all crowded around the screen.

"Garage door openers?" Ava said.

"That's right!" Genie Bob exclaimed. "You search the entire Internet and the thing I'm most famous for is a company that makes garage door openers."

"That's just sad, man," said William. "I feel your pain."

"Garage door openers are cool," David said. "I like to put water balloons underneath ours and crush them."

I wasn't sure if I was more surprised by the

fact that Genie Bob and Santa Claus went to school together, or the fact that a genie who had been trapped in a meteorite for thirteen million light years knew how to use a computer.

"It sounds to me like you're just jealous of Santa Claus and all his success," Ella said.

"Me? Jealous of that fat slob?" Bob snorted. "No way."

"May I say something?" asked Mrs. Walters. "This is all very interesting and we are sympathetic. But Mr. Bob here has given us a strict one-hour deadline to come up with a wish. I'm beginning to think he's just stalling for time to avoid granting it. So I propose we get back on task and talk about Mr. Bob's relationship with Santa Claus another day. And I hope you kids will wish for something that doesn't involve candy, trucks, giant bowls, or swimming pools."

She picked out the next index card.

WISH #4:

I WISH I COULD LIVE TO BE 100 YEARS OLD.

Huh! When I was trying to decide on my wish, I pretty much just made a list of stuff I wanted to *have*. It never occurred to me to wish for something else. Something you couldn't hold in your hand.

"That one was mine," said Ava in the front row.

"That's a *terrible* idea," William said.

"Why?" said Ava defensively.

"Lots of people already live to be a hundred years old," William said.

"My great-grandmother is a hundred and two," said Isabella. "And she still takes exercise classes twice a week."

"See? That proves my point," said William. "Why wish for something that you might get anyway? You're wasting the wish."

"Okay," Ava said, "then what if I wish to live *two* hundred years?"

"Well, that's a different story," Mrs. Walters said. "Nobody *ever* lived to be two hundred years old."

"It would be cool to do something nobody ever did in history," said David.

"Living two hundred years is an even *dumber* wish than wanting to live to be one hundred," William said. "If you live to be two hundred, you're going to be *old* for more than a hundred years."

"Some old people are healthy and happy," said Sophia.

"Yeah, and some are lying in a bed with no bladder or bowel control," said William. "You want to wish for a hundred years of *that*?"

"Okay, how about we wish to be young and healthy forever?" Ava said. "Or to live forever."

"Aha!" said Genie Bob. "The fountain of youth! An eternal quest. Peter Pan syndrome. Never grow up."

"I don't want to be young forever," Mia said.

"Why not?" Ava asked.

"You want to go to school for the rest of your life?" Mia replied.

Hmmm. I'd have to think that over.

"If we stay kids forever, we won't get our driver's licenses," Mia said. "We'll never vote. We'll never go to college, or move out of our parents' house. We'll never get married or have kids of our own. We'll never be in charge of anything."

"Yeah, but we'll never die of old age, either," Abigail said. "We'll never get gray and wrinkly and senile."

"My dad has hair growing out of his ears and nose," said Alyssa. "It's gross."

"My dad has to go to the bathroom, like, every fifteen minutes," Olivia said.

"See!" said Andrew. "Being young forever will be *great*! We'll never have to get a job and work for a living. We'll never have some mean boss tell us what to do. We'll always be taken care of."

"Oh, yeah? By who?" Mia asked. "Your parents aren't going to be around forever."

"Oh, just forget about it," Ava said. "But if you ask me, it would be a whole lot better to live forever than it would be to have something silly, like a lot of money or candy."

"I agree," Mrs. Walters said as she pulled the next index card out of the bowl.

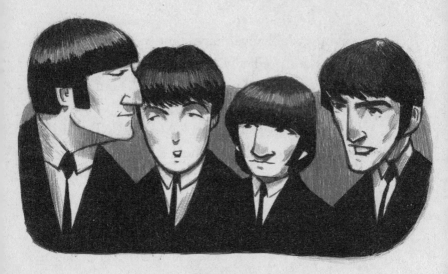

WISH #5:

I WISH THE BEATLES WOULD
GET BACK TOGETHER.

"Mine!" shouted Anthony.

"What?" Christopher asked. "You mean those disgusting bugs?"

"Are you kidding me?" Anthony asked. "You really don't know who the Beatles were? They were only the best rock and roll group in history."

"Never heard of 'em," said Christopher.

"My dad gave me a bunch of his old Beatles albums and I listened to them," Anthony said.

"They were great. But the Beatles broke up a long time ago."

"Wait a minute," Ella said. "Aren't some of those guys *dead*?"

"Yeah," Anthony said. "To fulfill my wish, they would have to come back to life. Can you do that, Genie Bob?"

"Piece of cake," Bob replied.

"That's creepy, bringing dead people back to life," said Sophia. "It seems immoral, or illegal, or something. It sounds like human cloning."

"But if we brought the Beatles back to life," Anthony said, "they would make more great music."

"How do *you* know?" Mia asked. "Maybe their new music would be *terrible*. They made all their records when they were young. If they made music now, it would be boring old dead-guy music."

"If we're going to bring somebody back from the dead, why bring back the Beatles?" asked Elizabeth. "Why not bring back Abraham Lincoln? He was a great man."

"Or we could bring back Martin Luther King Jr., John F. Kennedy, or Gandhi," suggested Hannah.

"Gandhi?" asked Christopher. "Who's *that*?"

"Some Indian dude," Logan said.

"If I was going to bring back somebody from the dead, I would bring back Mel Blanc," said Alex.

"Mel Blanc?" we all asked. "Who's he?"

"He was the guy who did the voices of Bugs Bunny, Daffy Duck, Porky Pig, Tweety Bird, and a bunch of other Looney Tunes characters," Alex told us. "He's my hero."

"One guy did all those voices?" asked Isabella.

"Yeah. Mel Blanc did Barney Rubble in *The Flintstones* too," Alex said. "Most people don't know that."

"And you want to bring *that* guy back from the dead instead of Abraham Lincoln?" asked Elizabeth.

"Well, yeah," Alex said. "Then we would have more Looney Tunes cartoons. When Mel Blanc died, all those characters died with him."

"You mean to tell me you can get any wish you want," asked Hannah, "and the best you can come up with is that you want to see more cartoons?"

"Well, I'd like to have a beach house too," Alex said.

"You kids are pathetic," said Genie Bob. "I hope the rest of ya came up with better wishes."

"Me too," said Mrs. Walters as she pulled out the next index card.

I WISH KIDS HAD THE RIGHT TO VOTE.

"That one was mine," said Olivia, who sits behind me. "I think it is totally unfair that we can't vote on Election Day."

"It's about time somebody made a *serious* wish," said Mrs. Walters.

"Olivia's right," said Elizabeth. "There are something like fifty million kids in this country. We make up a big percentage of the population, and grown-ups are always saying *we* are the future. A lot of decisions have a big impact on us.

And yet we have no say in how things are run. It's not fair."

"Remember that famous slogan they used in the Revolutionary War?" Mrs. Walters asked us. "We studied it last week."

"Give me liberty or give me death!" yelled Anthony.

"No, not that one," said Mrs. Walters.

"No taxation without representation," said Ava, all proud of herself.

"Yes, that one," said Mrs. Walters.

"Kids don't pay taxes," Ethan pointed out.

"Sure we do," Abigail said. "Every time I buy clothes or something at the mall, they add tax to the price."

"Well, you know, there's a perfectly good reason why kids can't vote," said Hannah.

"Why?" everybody asked.

"We don't *know* enough," Hannah said. "Do any of you read the papers or watch the news on TV?"

Elizabeth was the only one who raised her hand.

"See?" Hannah said. "How would kids know who to vote for?"

"Hey, not all grown-ups read the paper or

watch the news," said Ella. "There are millions of uninformed grown-ups, and *they* have the right to vote."

"Yeah," a few kids grumbled.

"What are they gonna do, say people can only vote if they follow the news?" asked William. "People can only vote if they're smart?"

"If kids were allowed to vote, you know who would be president of the United States?" asked Alex. "Miley Cyrus. Or Rihanna. Or the lead singer of some dumb boy band."

"I would vote for the quarterback of the Bears," Jacob said. "He would make a great president."

"See what I mean?" said Alex. "It would just be a big popularity contest."

"That's what elections are *anyway*," Hannah said. "Popularity contests. They're like *American Idol*, without the singing."

"I wouldn't want to vote *anyway*," said Christopher. "If we don't vote, they can't blame us for stuff that goes wrong."

"That's not a good attitude, Christopher," said Mrs. Walters. "Every citizen should vote."

"What's the big deal about voting?" Christopher said. "My dad told me that all politicians are liars. If you want to wish for something we aren't allowed to do, let's wish we could *drive*."

"That would be cool," David said.

"If I could drive, man, I would go a hundred miles an hour in my Lamborghini Gallardo Spyder," said Christopher. "Nobody would beat me."

"That's exactly why they don't let us drive," Ella said. "Because kids like you would go racing, get into accidents, and kill people."

"I would not!" Christopher insisted.

"You would too!" said Ella.

"All right, settle down everyone," Mrs. Walters said. "Let's move on, shall we? We're wasting valuable time."

WISH #7:

I WISH FOR A CLASS OF STUDENTS WHO ARE PERFECT ANGELS AND NEVER ARGUE OR ACT DISRESPECTFULLY.

"Hey, who made *that* dumb wish?" Logan asked.

"That one was mine, actually," Mrs. Walters said. "I thought I would throw it in for the heck of it."

"We want to wish for something *cool*," William said, and everybody agreed.

"That one doesn't count," Christopher said.

"Oh, well, at least I tried," Mrs. Walters said as she reached into the bowl and pulled out another index card.

WISH #7:

I WISH I COULD SLOW DOWN THE ROTATION OF THE EARTH.

"That's the dumbest thing I ever heard!" Logan exclaimed. "Who came up with that lame idea?"

"Let's be respectful of one another's wishes, please," Mrs. Walters warned Logan.

"That was *my* wish," said Natalie.

"Figures," Logan muttered.

Natalie is famous around school for thinking up weird stuff that doesn't exactly make sense. Like, one time we had a social studies test and instead of using a yellow marker to highlight all the important parts of the book, Natalie took a black marker to hide all the *unimportant* parts. She's either crazy or a genius. Maybe both.

"Tell us your thinking, Natalie," asked Mrs. Walters.

"Well, I figured that if we wished for money or some material object, we would just fight over who gets to keep it," Natalie explained. "But there's one thing that everybody wishes they had more of—time. There are only twenty-four hours in a day, right? And there are only three hundred sixty-five days in a year. But if the Earth rotated more slowly, or if it took longer to make a revolution around the sun, we would have more time."

"You're nuts," said Logan.

"Logan!" said Mrs. Walters.

"Actually, it makes sense," Ella said. "If a day was thirty hours long instead of twenty-four, we would have six more hours than we do now. That would mean six more hours to play, go online, hang out with your friends, or do anything you wanted to do."

"Six more hours to play ball!" said Jacob.

"Six more hours to shop!" said Abigail.

"It would also mean six more hours that our

parents could tell us to do chores around the house," Mia said, "or six more hours of homework."

"Six more hours we'd have to go to school," said Logan.

"Maybe it would be six more hours to sleep," Ella said. "I mean, we're still going to get tired, no matter how many hours there are in the day."

"I don't want to sleep more hours," Alyssa said. "I like things the way they are."

"Well, you could use the six hours any way you want," Natalie told Alyssa. "That's the beauty of it."

"I wish I *never* had to go to sleep," said Jacob. "I would play ball twenty-four/seven."

"If Natalie got her wish, we'd have to replace all our watches and clocks," Ella pointed out.

"If the Earth rotated more slowly, wouldn't it affect the weather and stuff?" asked Mia. "Like, the sun would be shining on the surface longer during the day, and nighttime would be longer too. So days would be hotter, and nights colder. Right, Mrs. Walters?"

"It makes sense," she replied.

"It might mess up the tides, too," Ashley said.

"And eclipses . . . communication satellites . . . cell phones . . . satellite TV . . ."

"Don't animals rely on astronomy to know when to migrate and hibernate and stuff?" Isabella asked. "They would get confused."

"Boo-hoo," said Logan. "We should worry about a bunch of confused animals?"

"Isn't it possible that if the Earth rotated more slowly, it could fall off its axis?" asked Mia. "Like a bicycle that stops rolling. Or it might fall out of its orbit around the sun and end up in another galaxy."

"That would be cool," David said.

"We could be messing with the entire space-time continuum!" exclaimed Ashley.

"I *told* you it was the dumbest wish I ever heard," Logan said.

"I hate to say it, but for once, Logan, you're right," Natalie said. "I respectfully withdraw the wish."

Genie Bob rolled his eyes. "This is gonna be a long day," he groaned.

Mrs. Walters reached into the bowl.

I WISH I COULD HAVE A GIGANTIC, FLAT-SCREEN, HIGH-DEFINITION TV THAT FILLS UP A WHOLE WALL IN MY ROOM.

"That would be cool," David said. "That's why I wished for it."

"It would be great to watch football games on a TV like that," said Jacob.

"How would you get it through the door?" asked Ella.

"Good point, Ella," said Mrs. Walters.

"You couldn't," David said. "It would have to be assembled inside my room."

"They don't even *make* TVs like that," Alyssa said.

"So what?" David replied. "It's a wish, right? I can wish for *anything*, even stuff that doesn't exist today."

"In that case," Natalie said, "why not wish for a room where the wall can disappear temporarily so you can bring the TV in, and then the wall can reappear afterward? Or how about a TV set that can go *through* walls?"

"You're nuts," said Logan, shaking his head.

"Logan!" said Mrs. Walters.

"Why not just wish for a movie theater in your house?" Ethan suggested. "Problem solved."

"I would be happy if I could just have a *regular* TV in my room," said Alyssa. "My parents won't let me."

"You should wish for new parents," Alex suggested.

"I would rather have my own amusement park than my own movie theater," William said.

"This is the same old story," said Hannah.

"One kid wishes for something for himself, and everybody else gets nothing. That's not fair."

"You could come over to my house to watch my awesome TV," David said.

"Gee, thanks!" said Hannah sarcastically.

"That's selfish," said Elizabeth. "I think we should wish for something *all* of us could enjoy instead of just one person."

"You kids are breakin' my heart," said Bob the genie.

"Okay," David said, "then let's wish for a big-screen TV for everybody in the class."

"I don't *want* a big-screen TV!" said Hannah.

"Anybody who wouldn't want a big-screen TV has mental problems," Logan said.

"Logan!" said Mrs. Walters. "Be respectful of other people's opinions."

"I really don't care how big my TV screen is," said Hannah. "What's important is the *content* of what you watch, not the size of the screen. Which would you rather watch, a bad TV show on a huge screen, or a great TV show on a little screen?"

"If a TV show is bad, I wouldn't want to watch it at *all*," said Anthony. "It doesn't matter how big the screen is."

"That's my point," said Hannah.

"I'm perfectly happy watching a TV show on my new iPod," said Abigail, who clearly wanted everybody to know she got a new iPod.

"The problem with a big-screen TV is that it makes *everything* bigger," said Ella. "That includes the bad stuff too. Like if somebody on TV has a big mole on their face or a weird-looking nose, it looks even weirder when it's five feet tall."

"That's why you don't see any weird-looking people on TV," said Madison.

"And that's why everybody on TV has plastic surgery," Abigail said.

"They do not," said Josh.

"Do too," Abigail said. "My sister told me—"

"Perhaps we can have that debate another day," Mrs. Walters interrupted. "We're running out of time!"

Genie Bob shook his head and laughed. He seemed to enjoy watching us argue.

"I hope the other wishes aren't just wishing for more *stuff*," Elizabeth said. "That's so superficial."

"Yeah, stuff doesn't make you happy," said Hannah.

"What's wrong with stuff?" asked Abigail. "I like stuff."

"Me too," said Christopher. "I wish I had all the stuff in the world."

"I wish for a new house for my mom because our house is falling apart," said Madison.

"I wish I had a fire-breathing lima bean with horns that can drive a race car," said Matthew.

"I wish I had a jet pack with a built-in frozen yogurt machine," said Alex.

"Enough!" Mrs. Walters shouted.

"Mrs. Walters," Madison said, "I'm not sure it will be possible to come up with a wish everybody in the class would want. We're all so different."

"We should wish for something everyone in the *world* would want," Hannah suggested. "Something that would make our planet a better place to live."

"Oh, brother!" William said. "Here we go again. Who do you want to save now? The polar bears?"

"How about we wish for Hannah to disappear?"

Logan said. "That's something everybody in the world would want."

"Logan!" said Mrs. Walters.

"Why not just wish for everybody in the world to have a big-screen TV?" David asked. "That would be cool."

"Millions of people around the world don't even have electricity in their houses!" Elizabeth told David. "Millions more don't even *have* houses."

"That's right," said Hannah. "Lots of people don't have a bowl of rice to fill their bellies. The last thing they need is a big-screen TV."

"Maybe if they had a big-screen TV," Logan said, "it would take their minds off the fact that they don't have any food."

"You're *repulsive!*" Hannah said. "I wish I lived in a world with no boys."

"Me too," said Elizabeth.

"I hate to tell you this, but if there were no boys in the world," said Josh, "the human race would die out."

"Eww, that's disgusting!" Hannah said.

"What did I say?" asked Josh.

"Enough!" said Mrs. Walters. "Be respectful,

all of you! I'll tell you what. David had a very interesting wish, and we respect him for it. But clearly, some members of the class are opposed to the idea. I'm sure we'll find something that will please everyone."

I looked up at the clock. It was a few minutes before two o'clock.

WISH #9:

I WISH WE COULD HAVE PERMANENT PEACE IN THE MIDDLE EAST.

Sophia raised her hand and said she chose that wish because she has relatives in Egypt.

"Excellent!" Mrs. Walters said. "People in the Middle East have been at war with one another for decades. Centuries, even. I can't imagine anyone would have an objection to that wish."

"I'd rather have a big-screen TV," David said.

"Me too," said Logan and Christopher.

"Wake me up when you kids decide," said Genie Bob, closing his eyes. "I'm gonna take a snooze."

"Why limit peace to the Middle East?" asked Elizabeth. "Why not go all the way and wish there were never any more wars? Between *anybody*."

"Amen," said Mrs. Walters, and a few kids chimed in with amens of their own.

"Fine with me," Sophia said.

"What if we got attacked?" Christopher said, "like on Pearl Harbor and 9/11. Are you saying we shouldn't fight back? We should just do nothing?"

"If we wished for permanent world peace, our country wouldn't *be* attacked," said Ella.

"Good point," Mrs. Walters said. "It would be great if there were no wars. And I like the fact that Sophia chose a wish that doesn't involve money, candy, or one of us getting something *personally*. That's very mature."

"You could argue that wishing for world peace *does* involve money," said Mia.

"How so?" asked Mrs. Walters.

"Well, if there was never any war," Mia said,

"a lot of grown-ups would lose their jobs."

"Like who?" asked Hannah.

"Like anybody who works for a company that makes fighter planes," said Mia. "Or a company that makes military uniforms, equipment, guns, ammunition, body armor, weapons, tanks, ships, boots, and all that other stuff the military needs. Those companies wouldn't be in business if there were no wars."

Huh! I never thought of *that*. There must actually be a lot of people who are *happy* when a war breaks out.

"My uncle is in the Marines," said Isabella. "If there were never any wars, would he be fired?"

"You can't be fired from the Marines," Ava said.

"But if there were no wars, we wouldn't need Marines anymore," Hannah pointed out. "Or Army, or Navy, or Air Force. We wouldn't need a military at all."

"Do you know that our country spends more than five hundred *billion* dollars every year for defense?" Elizabeth said. "That's more than the next thirty countries *combined*! Can you imagine what we could do with that money if we used it for education, health care, to clean up the environment, fix our roads and bridges, feed the hungry, house the homeless—"

"Oh, *please*," Logan said. "Time to save the world again!"

"You can wish for world peace all you want," said Ethan. "But there will always be dictators and crazy lunatics who want to kill us. That's just human nature. There have always been wars, and there always will be. The world is a dangerous place. That's why we have to spend so much money on defense."

"War is not human nature," Hannah said. "It's the nature of *man*. If women ran the world, it would be a different story. It's always men who start wars, you know, and commit violent crimes."

"Somebody should commit a violent crime against *you*," said Logan.

"Logan!" shouted Mrs. Walters.

"It doesn't matter who starts wars," Elizabeth said. "Wars are morally wrong. People who have jobs that are dependent on war should switch jobs. Why should anybody want to work for a company that makes something that kills people?"

"It's not so easy to just switch jobs," said Anthony. "My uncle lost his job six months ago and he still doesn't have a new one."

"War isn't the only thing that kills people, you know," Andrew pointed out. "My dad works for a supermarket that sells cigarettes. Cigarettes kill people. So should my dad quit his job because he works for a company that kills people?"

"No, your dad should tell the owner of the supermarket to stop selling cigarettes," Elizabeth said.

"Then the store would lose customers," said Andrew. "Smokers would just go to another supermarket to get their cigarettes."

"Cigarettes should be illegal anyway if they kill people," said Hannah. "They shouldn't be sold in *any* stores."

"That's right," a few kids agreed.

"Hey, alcohol kills lots of people," Olivia pointed out. "Are you saying they should ban that, too?"

"Yes!" Hannah said. "Then there would be no more drunk drivers."

"Actually, alcohol *was* illegal for twelve years starting in 1920," Mrs. Walters told us. "But people started making their own liquor, and organized crime families got rich selling it."

"I saw an article that said adults should drink a glass of wine every day to prevent heart disease," said Ava. "So drinking alcohol in moderation doesn't kill people. It can be *good* for you."

"Even if it did kill people, you don't just go and ban everything that ever killed anybody," said Josh. "A guy who lived down my street died in a snowmobile accident a few years ago. So should we ban snowmobiles?"

"This is a free country," said Christopher. "People should be free to buy whatever they want, even if it kills 'em. As long as they don't hurt anybody *else*. Isn't that the whole idea of freedom and America and stuff?"

"Why are we talking about this?" asked Sophia. "I just wished for no more wars."

"I think the point is that wars, smoking, drinking, and so on all hurt people in various ways," said Mrs. Walters. "But if we get rid of all those things, people who are dependent on them for their living would suffer."

"You could say that about anything, really," said Natalie. "If we wished for people to never get sick anymore, it would put all the doctors out of business. Nurses and hospitals and medical equipment companies too."

"If we wished for cars to never break down, it would put all the auto mechanics out of business," Christopher said. "And the car manufacturers too, because if cars never broke down, nobody would need to buy a new one."

"If we get rid of *anything* in the world, we'll actually be hurting a lot of other people," said Ella. "I don't want to be responsible for that."

"We could discuss this all day," Mrs. Walters said. "Perhaps we should move on and see what other wishes people came up with."

"Good idea," said Genie Bob, opening his eyes. "By the time you brats finally make a decision, Christmas will be over."

WISH #10:

I WISH I WOULD WIN THE LOTTERY.

Alyssa, who sits in the back row, raised her hand.

"That would be cool," said David.

"I'm sorry," Mrs. Walters told Alyssa. "I'm going to make an executive decision and disqualify this wish."

"Why?" asked Alyssa.

"Lotteries are a form of gambling," said Mrs. Walters, "and gambling is illegal for kids. In some parts of the country, it's illegal for *everybody*."

"It's just the same as my wish anyway," Abigail pointed out. "Wishing to win the lottery is just like wishing for a million dollars."

"No, it's not," said Hannah. "It's even *worse*. Because if Alyssa won the lottery, she would be depriving the person who *would* have won millions of dollars. So Alyssa would be wishing for something good to happen to her at the expense of some other person."

"Interesting," said Mrs. Walters. "It shows you have empathy for other people, Hannah."

"Whatever that is," said Logan.

"I've heard that people who win lotteries are usually unhappy afterward," Mia said. "Their friends and family argue over the money. People try to rip them off. Or they can't handle the sudden fame and fortune."

"I bet I could handle it," said Andrew.

"I heard about some guy in Texas who won a thirty-million-dollar lottery," said Ethan. "Billie

Bob something or other. It ruined his life. Two years later, he killed himself."

"Wow!" everybody said.

"It's out of the question," Mrs. Walters said as she pulled out the next wish. "Sorry, Alyssa. No lotteries."

I WISH I COULD PLAY SHORTSTOP
FOR THE YANKEES.

Nobody was surprised when Jacob jumped up and started high-fiving and fist-bumping everybody. We all knew his wish would have something to do with sports. That's all he lives for.

"The Yankees stink," I told Jacob. "You should play for the Cubs. The Cubs rule."

"The Cubs stink," Jacob replied. "They haven't won a World Series in a hundred years!"

"Boys!" said Mrs. Walters.

"If I got my wish, I would get to play baseball *all* the time," Jacob said. "I would be famous. People would cheer for me and I'd earn millions of dollars. Kids would be asking me for autographs. It would be a great life."

"That would be cool," David said.

"No offense, kid, but you're ten years old," Genie Bob told Jacob. "If you played for the Yankees, the Yankees would be terrible. Especially with you at short. They put the best glove man at short."

Glove man? I couldn't believe that a genie who had been traveling around in space for thousands of years would know how to talk baseball.

"What I meant to say was that I wish I was *good enough* to play for the Yankees," Jacob said.

"Well, that's a different wish," said Genie Bob. "Ya gotta be real specific when you're making a potentially life-changing wish like this."

"Is there any downside to Jacob's wish?" asked Mrs. Walters.

I looked behind at Mia. She was sure to find a cloud behind every silver lining. But for once, she kept her mouth shut.

"Yeah," said William. "The rest of us get *nothing*."

"You'd get to watch me play," Jacob said.

"On my awesome big-screen TV," David added.

"Gee, thanks," William muttered.

"Are you aware that the average baseball player's career lasts only five to seven years?" Ava asked. "I looked it up. With football players, it's even shorter. Like two to four years."

I didn't doubt her, because Ava knows all kinds of useless information like that. She probably memorized the whole Internet.

"Five years on the Yankees would be awesome," Jacob said.

"It's better to be famous for five years than not to be famous at all," said Andrew.

"What would you do with yourself for the rest of your life?" Mia asked Jacob. "You'd be a has-been. Washed up at fifteen."

"I'd go to card shows and sign pictures of myself," Jacob said. "That's what all the old-timers do. They make a lot of money."

"I would think it would be tough to go back to being a normal kid after you've been really famous," said Madison. "Like all those child stars on TV. They usually get messed up with drinking or drugs or they go crazy."

"You know, some ballplayers have careers that last a long time," Jacob told us. "Babe Ruth played for twenty-two years."

"And some have careers that last *one* year," Ava said. "Five years was an *average*."

"My coach told me about this guy named Rufus Meadows," Jacob told us. "He was on the Cincinnati Reds in 1926. Meadows pitched to *one* batter in *one* game. That was it. His whole career."

"Being a pro athlete isn't all that great, you know," Mia said. "They travel all the time, so they have to be away from their family a lot. They get injured, too."

"What if you played for the Yankees, but you weren't that good?" asked Alyssa.

"Oh, I'd be good," Jacob said. "I'd be awesome."

"What if you were really good, but you made one really bad play?" I asked Jacob. "Like that guy Bill Buckner. He was a really good player, but he let a ground ball go between his legs and cost the Red Sox the World Series."

I saw a video about that. It happened back in the 1980s, but when you say the name Bill Buckner, the only thing anybody remembers about him was that he booted a ground ball.

"That wouldn't happen to me," Jacob said.

"I'll bet Buckner didn't think it would happen to him, either," I told him.

"I'll *wish* for it not to happen to me," Jacob said.

"One wish per customer," said Genie Bob. "No exceptions. No freebies."

"Okay, okay!" Jacob said. "I hear everything all of you are saying. I *get* it. There would be a downside to playing in the big leagues. Stuff could go wrong. I could get injured. But I would still do it. Playing shortstop for the Yankees has been my fantasy ever since I was little."

"Can't argue with that," said Genie Bob. "Ya gotta follow your dreams, kid."

"Of course, it wouldn't do the rest of us any good," said Ashley.

"True," said Mrs. Walters. "Let's move on, shall we? We're not even halfway through our wishes."

WISH #12:

I WISH CARS RAN ON WATER.

Huh?

Everybody turned around to see who dreamed up *that* crazy idea.

"Why would you want to drive a car on water?" asked William.

"We already have cars that run on water," Alex said. "They're called *boats*."

"No!" Elizabeth said. "What I meant was that I wish we had cars that could use water for *fuel.* As a power source. Instead of gasoline, you know?"

"Oh, that's different," Alex said.

"Think of it," said Elizabeth. "If cars ran on water, we wouldn't have to import oil from the Mideast. We wouldn't have to be nice to all those oil-producing countries that hate us. We wouldn't have to fight wars over oil or worry about what happens when the oil is all gone. There would be no pollution or global warming, because we wouldn't have to burn oil and give off greenhouse gasses. We wouldn't have to drill in areas that threaten wildlife. There would be no oil spills. It would save the planet."

"You wouldn't have to go to the gas station to fill up your tank, either," said Sophia. "You could just attach a hose from the outside of your house and run it straight into your car's gas tank. I mean, water tank."

"That would be cool," said David.

"You wouldn't have to worry about running out of gas, either," said Josh. "You can always get some water."

"People wouldn't have to pay so much money to fill up," Ella said.

"Hey, if you were really thirsty, you could just siphon some water out of your tank and drink it," said Alex. "We wouldn't have to carry around water bottles."

Everybody was getting really excited about the idea of having cars that run on water.

"It's a *very* interesting wish, Elizabeth," Mrs. Walters said. "I think we should consider this one seriously."

"Can I say something?" asked Christopher.

Christopher doesn't talk a whole lot, so everybody turned around to see what he had to say.

"My uncle owns a garage," he said, "and I know a lot about cars. The car moves because a little bit of gas ignites and the explosion pushes the piston in the engine. You can't ignite water. Water can't make a car go."

"It's a *wish*, Christopher!" Elizabeth said. "If you're wishing, *anything* is possible. Right, Genie Bob?"

"Right-ee-oh."

"Wait a minute. Has anybody considered the fact that water is *scarce*?" Hannah asked. "We have water shortages all the time. Half the people in the world don't have enough water to *drink*."

"Oh, here we go again," Logan moaned. "Get out the violins."

"How can we even *think* about cars that run on water when there are people dying because they don't have clean drinking water?" asked Hannah.

"Hannah is right," said Elizabeth. "Cancel my wish. It's Christmastime, remember? We should wish for clean drinking water for everyone in the world. That would be a worthwhile wish for the holidays."

"Why is it that you two always worry about poor people and starving people instead of yourselves?" Logan asked. "Why don't you look out for yourselves for once?"

"Because Elizabeth and I are not selfish people, that's why," said Hannah. "Why is it that *you* always look out for yourself and never for the rest of the world?"

"I'm looking out for the rest of the world," Logan said. "This is how I see it. If I look out for my own interests, then I'm gonna be successful and happy. And if *everyone* looked out for their own interests, then *everyone* would be successful and happy. If somebody isn't successful, that just means they weren't looking out for their own interests."

A few kids were nodding their heads.

"That just sounds like an excuse for being selfish," Elizabeth said.

"Hey, it's human nature to protect yourself," Logan said. "Do you think when a lion is in the jungle, it worries about some endangered species before it kills its dinner? No, it only cares about itself."

"I hate to break the news to you, but lions aren't human," Hannah told Logan. "So maybe you can come up with a better example of human nature."

"You know what I *mean*," said Logan. "It's human nature to protect yourself. That's a fact."

"Well, I think it's human nature to protect the human race and the planet we live on too," said Elizabeth. "And if we don't conserve our water supplies, there will *be* no human race."

"You know, it's not fair to say everybody would be successful and happy if they simply looked after their own interests," Hannah said. "What about people who have a disease, or they're handicapped, or they got into an accident?

What about people who live in a city that got flooded by a tsunami? What do you say to them? *Tough? Too bad? Better luck next time?*"

"If a tsunami flooded somebody's city," said Alex, "I'd say they could use a car that ran on water."

"This discussion, just like a car that runs on water, is getting us nowhere," said Mrs. Walters. "Perhaps we should move on to the next wish."

"We've only got about twenty minutes left," I told everybody. "If we don't hurry up we're going to miss Christmas vacation!"

WISH #13:

I WISH IT WAS CHRISTMAS ALL YEAR LONG. AND EVERY DAY WAS MY BIRTHDAY.

"That one is mine," said Ashley. "Everybody would be happy all the time, because everybody's happy at Christmas and birthday time. You don't have to worry about anything."

"Not only that," Abigail said, "but we would

get presents all year long! We'd have a Christmas tree up in my house every day of the year."

"No, the best part would be that we would have snow all year round," said Jacob. "I could go snowboarding in July!"

"That would be cool," said David.

"But if it was Christmas all year long, Christmas would lose its meaning," Mia said. "It wouldn't be special. Holidays are so nice because they only come around once a year."

"Do you have to look at the bad side of everything?" Logan asked.

"Every positive thing has a negative side," said Mia. "It would be better to think about the negative side now than after we make the wish, right?"

I had to admit she made sense.

"It just occurred to me," Elizabeth said, "if we had snow all year round, we'd have to worry about global *cooling* instead of global warming. It could lead to another ice age."

"Oh, brother!" said Logan.

"Okay, forget about Christmas," Ashley said. "What about having your birthday every day?"

"That would be cool," said David.

"I know you're just going to call me a party pooper," Mia said, "but if every day was your birthday, you would probably be dead within three months."

"Party pooper!" shouted Logan.

"How do you figure that, Mia?" Ashley asked.

"Well, if you had a birthday every day, in one month you'd be thirty years old," Mia explained. "In two months, you'd be sixty. In three months, you'd be ninety. And you're ten years old now, so that's a hundred. You'd grow old really fast. Chances are, you'd be dead three months from now."

"I never thought of it that way," Ashley said. "I just figured I'd get presents every day, people would bake me cakes all the time, and everybody would always be nice to me."

"Oh, they'll be real nice to you," said Logan, "especially when you're an old, senile, wrinkled ten-year-old."

"It was a dumb idea," Ashley said. "Tear that one up, Mrs. Walters."

WISH #14:

I WISH I HAD A DOG.

Everybody turned and looked at Isabella. We all knew that had to be her wish, because she loves animals. She always says she wants to be a veterinarian when she grows up.

"Don't you already have, like, a dozen pets at home?" asked Madison.

"I have two cats, a bunny, a parakeet, a hermit crab, two turtles, and some fish," Isabella said. "But I don't have a dog."

"So go to an animal shelter or a pet shop and get a dog," said Ethan. "Problem solved. What's the big deal?"

"I'm allergic to dogs," Isabella said.

Oh.

"Ah, it's the same old story," said Genie Bob. "Humans always want what they can't have. If you were allergic to elephants, you'd want an elephant."

"I would not," Isabella said.

"Where would you keep an elephant, anyway?" asked Alex. "I guess you could wish for an elephant house in your backyard. But on second thought, you only get one wish. So if Isabella wished for an elephant house, she wouldn't get the elephant. And what would you do with the elephant house if you didn't have an elephant to put in it?"

"I don't want an elephant!" Isabella yelled. "I want a dog."

"I believe there are some breeds of dogs that people aren't allergic to," said Mrs. Walters. "You might want to look into that, Isabella."

"Instead of wishing for a dog, why don't you just wish there were no such things as dog allergies?" Ella asked Isabella. "Then you wouldn't be allergic to dogs and you could just get any dog you want."

"Good idea, Ella," said Mrs. Walters.

"Look, anybody can get a dog," said Alex. "But nobody can get a *talking* dog. Let's wish for *that*. If my dog, Bella, could talk, I could have a regular conversation with her."

"Talking animals are cool," said David.

"I think part of the reason why animals are lovable is because they *can't* talk," said Olivia.

"Parrots are lovable, and they talk," said Ella.

"If animals could talk," Mia said, "some of them would be annoying. Just like some people are annoying when they talk. I don't think I need to name any names."

"You know what?" Logan said. "*You're* annoying. Why don't you shut up?"

"Would you like to go the the principal's office, Logan?" asked Mrs. Walters.

"No."

"What if your dog could talk and it told you that it hated you?" asked Ashley. "That would be a royal bummer."

"I wish I had a *flying* dog," Alex said. "A flying dog that talked."

"That would be cool," said David.

"I wish I had a pet dragon that would take me to a magical rainbow," said Madison.

"I wish I had a unicorn that would fly me anywhere," said Natalie.

"I wish I had my own zoo all to myself," said Isabella. "I could have every species in the world there."

"Have fun cleaning *that* up every day," said Alex.

"I wish I was a squirrel," William said. "I would be able to climb trees really easily."

"And get hit by cars really easily," said Alex.

"I wish I was a flying hamster," David said.

Everybody turned to look at David, because we all had the same question.

"Why would you want to be a flying hamster?"

"It would be cool," David said.

"Next!" said Mrs. Walters.

WISH #15:

I WISH THAT THE WORLD WAS A BETTER PLACE. WITH NO POVERTY. NO LITTER. NO POLLUTION. NO CANCER. NO HIGH GAS PRICES. NO WARS. NO RACISM. NO GLOBAL WARMING. NO DISEASES. NO CRIME. NO DRUGS. NO CHILD IN THE WORLD GOING TO BED HUNGRY AT NIGHT. AND EVERYBODY WAS HAPPY ALL THE TIME. AND I WISH MY BROTHER WOULD STOP THROWING HIS UNDERWEAR AT ME.

We all knew whose wish it was, because Hannah took about ten minutes to write it all down. And she's also one of these people who's always talking about doing good things for poor people and saving the world and stuff.

"That's very altruistic of you, Hannah," said Mrs. Walters. "Does anybody know what that word means?"

Nobody raised a hand. Not even Ava, and she knows *everything*.

"Altruism means unselfish concern for the welfare of others," Mrs. Walters told us.

"You mean, like being a sap?" asked Logan.

"No, Logan," said Mrs. Walters. "I mean, like caring about people other than yourself."

"I hate to bust your bubble, kids, but that's a multiple wish," Genie Bob said. "Ya can't just make a list of wishes, put commas between 'em, and call 'em one wish. That's the same thing as wishing for more wishes."

"You gotta hand it to her for trying," Alex said.

"Choose *one* wish," ordered Genie Bob.

"Why?" asked Hannah.

"Because those are the rules, that's why,"

said Genie Bob. "And I make the rules. Sheesh! Nobody ever grants *me* any wishes, y'know. There aren't any perks that come with this job. Boy, I wish I could have just one wish. I would quit this genie gig in a second."

"This isn't about *you*," Mrs. Walters told Genie Bob. "My class gets the wish, remember?"

"Maybe you should tackle the underwear problem," Alex told Hannah. "That seems doable."

"So, we can have any wish in the world," said Elizabeth, "and you think we should wish that Hannah's brother would stop throwing his underwear at her? Oh yeah, that makes a *lot* of sense."

"It was a *joke*!" Alex said. "Lighten up."

"If I just wish to end poverty in the world, then there will still be people who get horrible diseases," Hannah complained. "And if I wish that there were no horrible diseases, then there will still be drugs and crime and global warming and all those other serious problems."

"These are the kinds of decisions that our political leaders have to make every day," Mrs. Walters told us. "There are a lot of problems in the world, and we can't solve all of them at the same time, or all of them by ourselves."

"Why not?" Hannah asked. "I thought we could wish for *anything*."

"Sorry," Genie Bob said. "Even in the wish community, life ain't always fair."

"But I can't decide which one to wish for," Hannah said.

"Neither can I," said Mrs. Walters, as she reached into the bowl for the next card.

WISH #16:

I WISH I COULD SPEAK SPANISH.

"That one's mine," said Madison. "My family took a trip to Mexico last summer, and I couldn't communicate with the people there. Spanish sounds like such a beautiful language, so I wish I could speak it."

"You know, next year when you kids are in sixth grade you're going to start learning foreign languages," said Mrs. Walters. "You can take Spanish then, Madison."

"Yeah, but that will involve a lot of work," Madison said. "I don't want to spend years. I want to be fluent *tomorrow*. I want to snap my fingers and be able to speak Spanish."

"Why don't you just wish you could speak *every* language?" said Josh. "I mean, if you're gonna wish, wish big. That's what I say."

"I'll tell you what I wish," said William. "I wish we *didn't* have to learn another language in school next year."

"Yeah, what do we need *that* for?" said Logan. "I'm not going anywhere. I like things right here in the good old U.S. of A."

"Everybody should speak American," said Christopher.

"American isn't a *language*," Hannah said, shaking her head. "We speak *English*."

"Well, those people in England ripped off our language," Christopher said. "That's why we had to go kick their butts in 1776."

I was going to tell Christopher what a dope he is, but I didn't want Mrs. Walters to tell me I need to respect other people's opinions no matter how dumb they are.

"Learning another language makes you a

broader, more interesting person," said Mrs. Walters.

"I'm plenty interesting right now," William said.

"Isn't it confusing to learn more than one language?" asked Mia. "Wouldn't you get them mixed up in your head?"

"Oh, no, not at all," Mrs. Walters said. "There are people who speak dozens of languages."

"Why don't we vote on it?" asked Alyssa.

"Fair enough," Mrs. Walters said. "All in favor of wishing to speak Spanish, raise your hands."

Madison and a few other kids put their hands up.

"All opposed, raise your hands," Mrs. Walters said.

Most of the rest of us raised our hands. Some kids didn't vote for either option.

"Sorry, Madison," said Mrs. Walters.

WISH #17:

I WISH I HAD A TIME MACHINE.

"Yeah!" a bunch of us exclaimed.

"That one was mine," Ethan said. "If I had a time machine, I could travel back to any period in history. I could meet Abraham Lincoln or George Washington. I could see how the ancient Egyptians built the pyramids. Nobody knows, y'know."

"Having a time machine would be cool," David said.

"And of course," Ethan added, "I would take you guys with me, so it wouldn't be a wish just for *me*. It would be for *all* of us."

"That's very altruistic of you, Ethan," said Mrs. Walters.

"If I had a time machine, I would go back five years so I could be a little kid again," said Ashley. "Life was simpler when we were little."

"I would go back to the Sixties and prevent the assassinations of John F. Kennedy and Martin Luther King Jr.," said Hannah.

"If I had a time machine," said Natalie, "I wouldn't travel to the past. I'd go to the *future*. Then I could see what I'm going to be like as a grown-up, where I'll live, what job I'll have, what my family will look like."

"You'd be able to see all the next-generation video game systems and cool technology they'll have too," said William.

"Like flying cars and stuff," added Christopher.

"And you could see who is going to win the Super Bowl that year," said Jacob. "Then you could come back and bet on it and win a lot of money."

"I don't think that would be legal," said Mrs. Walters.

"How would anyone catch you?" asked Jacob.

"I saw this movie once about a guy who goes back in time and accidently kills his mother," Natalie said. "So she never gave birth to him, and he didn't really exist anymore."

"That makes no sense at all," said Logan.

"But Natalie makes a good point," said Mrs. Walters. "If you traveled back in time, you would have to be very careful. Because anything you do in the past could change everything that happens after that point in time."

"I'd make sure not to kill my mom," Alex said.

"But what if you were walking down the street and you happened to kick a seed with your foot," said Natalie, "and years later that seed grew into a tall tree. And the tall tree got struck by lightning and fell on a house. And it just happened to be, say, Thomas Edison's childhood home. And he was killed when the tree crashed into his bedroom. And he never grew up to invent the lightbulb. We would be sitting here in the dark right now. And it would be *your* fault because you kicked that little seed."

"You have a sick mind," said Logan.

"Logan!" said Mrs. Walters.

"I guess the moral to the story," said Alex, "is not to kick seeds."

"If I was going to wish for a machine it wouldn't be a time machine," said Christopher. "I'd wish for a machine that did my homework for me automatically."

"That would be cool," said David.

"I'm not sure I would approve of that," Mrs. Walters said.

"Why not just wish that we didn't *have* homework in the first place?" asked Ella. "Then you wouldn't need a machine to do it for you."

"What's wrong with homework?" asked Madison. "Doing homework is how we learn things."

Everybody turned around and looked at Madison. Obviously, she had lost her mind.

"If I was going to wish for a machine," said Natalie, "I would wish for a pencil that allows you to draw things that become real as you need them. Like, you could draw a picture of a house, and then a real house that looks just like it would appear in front of you."

"If I was going to wish for a machine," said Abigail, "I would wish for a machine that turns dirt into gold. Then I'd make a fortune."

"If you could turn dirt into gold, gold would become worth nothing because there would be so much of it," claimed Mia. "Gold is valuable because it's rare."

"Yeah," said Alex, "but if you turned dirt into gold and the gold was worth nothing, you could make a fortune selling dirt."

"Why don't we just wish for a magical machine that can do *anything* we want it to do?" suggested Natalie.

"How about just going with my original idea?" said Ethan. "A time machine."

"Speaking of time," said Genie Bob, "you only have ten minutes left. Looks like you're going to miss your Christmas vacation."

"Let's hurry," said Mrs. Walters. "We need to get through everyone's wishes."

WISH #18:

I WISH I HAD SUPERPOWERS.

"Yeah!" a bunch of us exclaimed.

"Mine," claimed Josh, raising his hand.

"Sorry, dude, but you need to be more specific," Genie Bob told Josh. "If ya simply tell me you want superpowers, I might give you the power to eat a ton of broccoli, or the power to lick your own elbow, which, by the way, is impossible for humans."

Genie Bob licked his elbow. We all tried to lick ours. He was right. Impossible.

"Okay," Josh said, thinking it over. "I need to pick one superpower? That's a no-brainer. I wish I could fly. Like, on a flying carpet. I wish I could jump up to the sky and stay there and relax on the clouds."

"That would be cool," said David.

"Yeah!" we all agreed. Of all the superpowers, nothing could possibly be better than flying.

"Big mistake," Genie Bob told us. "Believe me, *everybody* wishes they could fly. I get that wish *all* the time. But ya know what happened the last time somebody wished they could fly? The poor guy crashed into a plate glass window and landed on a fence. Believe me, ya don't want to wish that on anybody. Things are dangerous enough as it is without the sky being filled with flying people."

"How about superstrength?" suggested Abigail. "Then I could crush a piece of coal in my bare hands like Superman and turn it into a diamond."

"Why not just wish for a box full of diamonds?" said Ella. "Avoid the middleman."

"Is that all people care about?" asked Hannah. "Money? Diamonds? Buying things?"

"I would rather have X-ray vision," suggested Matthew. "Then I could see through walls."

"I never understood the big attraction of seeing through walls," said Alex. "You can just walk through the door and see what's on the other side of the wall with your *regular* vision."

"I would wish for superhearing," suggested Ashley. "Then I could hear what people are whispering about me."

"You would also pick up every conversation people are having miles away," said Mia. "You'd hear every bird chirp, every door creak, every time somebody sneezed. You wouldn't be able to sleep at night. Superhearing would probably drive you insane."

"I wish that I had the power to communicate with ghosts," said Anthony, "and to bring dead people back to life."

"That's just weird," Alyssa said, "and creepy."

I guess the wheels were turning in our heads, because everybody started suggesting superpowers they wish they had. Kids wished they could be invisible, invulnerable, or able to read minds. Jacob wished he could run really fast so he would be the greatest athlete in the world. Olivia loves to swim, and she said she wished she could breathe underwater. Andrew wished he could control the weather. Isabella wished she could create clones of herself and morph them into animals. Alex wished he had heat vision so he could toast marshmallows at any time. And me, well, I wished I could walk up walls like Spider-Man.

"Man, you kids are greedy!" Genie Bob said, "I hate to rain on your parade, but this ain't no grocery store. You don't come to me with a list and pick stuff off the shelves. You get one superpower, and that's all."

"You know, for a genie, you're really not all that nice," said Sophia.

"Yeah, go ahead and complain," Genie Bob said. "Maybe the *next* time a meteorite crashes into your class and a genie pops out, he'll be nicer than I am."

"There's no need to get snippy about it," said Mrs. Walters as she pulled the next index card out of her jar.

WISH #19:

I WISH MY PARENTS WOULD GET BACK TOGETHER.

When Mrs. Walters read that card, nobody jumped up to say it was theirs. We were all looking at each other nervously. Then, finally, Ella raised her hand in the back corner of the room.

"I didn't know we were going to say out loud who made each wish," Ella said. "I would have chosen another one."

"That's okay, Ella," Mrs. Walters said. "How

many of you have a family in which Mom and Dad are no longer together?"

About ten kids raised their hand. So did Mrs. Walters.

"At least I'm not the only one," Ella said. "My parents just got separated a few weeks ago."

"I'm so sorry, Ella," Mrs. Walters said. "I know how difficult that can be. My parents split up when I was about your age."

"My parents split up *twice*," said Andrew. "First my dad left after my folks weren't getting along. Then they went through counseling and he moved back home. But then they got along even worse and he moved out again. They get along better now than they did when they were together."

"That happens sometimes," Mrs. Walters said. "In some cases it's *good* for two people to split up because they just can't get along."

"I still wish my parents were together again," Ella said. She looked like she might cry.

"I wish I had a brother or sister," said Isabella. "I'm an only child."

"I wish I had *no* brothers or sisters," said Alex. "There are five kids in my family, and I'm the youngest."

"I wish I could meet my real mother and father," said Alyssa. "I was adopted."

"I wish my mother was still alive," Mrs. Walters said.

It was quiet in the room. I guess everybody had some kind of unusual relationship in their family that they were thinking about. My uncle got in trouble last year, and he was in jail for a while, but I didn't say anything about it.

"There's no such thing as a perfect family," Mrs. Walters told us. "How about this? Let's all agree to be supportive and respectful of each other. And if one of us ever needs to talk to someone, we'll be there for them."

"Yeah," we all agreed.

"For now, let's move on," said Mrs. Walters.

WISH #20:

I WISH FOR A PLANE TICKET TO SOUTH DAKOTA BECAUSE I WOULD BE ABLE TO SEE WILD BUFFALO AND WALK IN THE MOUNTAINS.

"Me!" William jumped up and proudly claimed credit.

"They have wild buffalo in South Dakota?" asked Mrs. Walters.

"I saw it in a comic book once," William said.

"Your wish is for a *plane ticket*?" said Josh. "Are you kidding me? Why don't you wish for your own private jet? Then you can go anywhere you want, whenever you want."

"I'm sure everyone here has a special place they would like to go," said Mrs. Walters.

"I would wish for an all-expense-paid trip to Pluto," said Christopher.

"The temperature on Pluto is minus 369 degrees," Ava pointed out. "Your body would be frozen solid in about a second. And there's no air, either."

"Then I would wish for a heated space suit," Christopher said.

"I wish I could go to the moon," said Anthony.

"That would be cool," David said.

"I've been to the moon," Genie Bob said. "It's way overrated. Big bore. Nothin' going on there. Believe me, ya don't want to go to the moon."

"I wish there was a magical place where no one could go but me," said Madison. "Nobody could tell me what to do. The flowers would gleam and there would be a wide open field. And pixies would fly over your head."

"Pixies?" we all said.

"Why are we arguing over where we wish we could go?" said Ethan. "Why don't we just wish for the whole class to have the power to teleport wherever we want? Like on *Star Trek*. That would be even better than a time machine."

"If everyone in the world had that power," said Hannah, "we wouldn't need cars, trains, planes, or ships. We wouldn't need to burn gas. There would be no global warming."

"And we would save so much *time*," Natalie said. "Can you imagine if you could go from New York to California in seconds?"

"That would be cool," said David.

"My mom works for an airline," said Mia. "She would lose her job."

"*Everyone* in the travel industry would lose their jobs," Ella said.

"My dad is a truck driver," said Christopher. "Would he lose his job?"

"Sure," Mia said. "If we could teleport stuff, we wouldn't need the travel industry, shipping companies, the post office, railroads, highways. It would be a different world."

"Isn't it kind of risky for us to make a decision

that would change the world so dramatically?" asked Ashley.

"We would be changing it for the *better*," insisted Ethan.

"Maybe we would be changing it for the worse," said Mia. "You don't know. We can't predict what might happen."

"Teleportation!" exclaimed Ethan. "What's the debate? It would be like the invention of the lightbulb, or the airplane."

"If it weren't for the airplane, there would be no 9/11, no Hiroshima, no Pearl Harbor," said Mia.

"Oh, give me a break!" said Ethan. "Are you gonna claim the plane is a bad thing because there have been some tragedies involving planes? You can say that about *anything*. "If we didn't have water, nobody would ever drown. So should we get rid of water?"

"Water is a necessity," Mia pointed out. "Airplanes aren't."

"Christmas vacation . . . ," Bob said, rolling his eyes. "Slipping away . . ."

Mrs. Walters picked the next card out of the bowl.

WISH #21:

I WISH I HAD MY OWN REALITY TV SHOW
AND I WAS REALLY FAMOUS SO I LIVED
IN A MANSION AND RULED THE WORLD
WHERE I COULD CONTROL THUNDER.
LIGHTNING. AND RAIN.

"That one's me, baby!" said Andrew, jumping up to high-five Logan.

"You are such an egomaniac," said Elizabeth.

"You know it!" Andrew said proudly.

"It wasn't a compliment," Elizabeth said. "Egomaniacs are selfish jerks who think the whole world revolves around them."

"You're just jealous because you can't control the weather like me," Andrew said.

"Why don't you get over yourself?" Hannah told Andrew. "If you want to be famous so badly, why don't you do something *great*? Invent something. Cure cancer. Create a brilliant piece of art or music. *Accomplish* something. Then you'll be famous."

"Paris Hilton never accomplished anything," Abigail pointed out. "She was born famous."

"Children, children!" said Mrs. Walters.

"Famous people aren't necessarily happy, you know," said Mia.

"That's true," Ashley said. "A lot of them are lonely, pathetic people."

"Yeah," Andrew said, "but they're lonely, pathetic, *famous* people."

"You know, if you were famous, people would be pestering you for autographs all the time," said Mia. "You wouldn't even be able to go out to eat in a restaurant, because people would come over and bother you."

"I would hire bouncers to beat up people who bother me," Andrew said. "And I would have flunkies sign my autograph for me so I wouldn't have to."

"You can't do that," said Ella. "People want a real autograph."

"And if you're famous," Mia said, "the paparazzi will be chasing you around trying to take your picture all the time."

"Let 'em," Andrew said as he struck a pose. "I love getting my picture taken."

"The paparazzi chased Princess Diana into a tunnel and her car crashed," said Abigail. "That's how she died."

"No it isn't," Ava said. "She crashed because her driver was *drunk*."

"Some people are famous for the wrong reason," said Ashley. "Like John Wilkes Booth. He's famous because he assassinated Abraham Lincoln. You don't want to be famous like *that*."

"Yeah," said Alyssa. "Then there's Hitler, Al Capone, Lee Harvey Oswald. . . ."

"The Hamburglar," added Alex.

"Who's the Hamburglar?" asked Christopher.

"He's that guy who steals hamburgers from Ronald McDonald," Alex told him.

"That guy ain't famous," said Christopher.

"Okay, I think we've established that fame can have its drawbacks," said Mrs. Walters. "Let's hurry. There are only a few more wishes left and it's almost two-thirty."

WISH #22:

I WISH I COULD EAT ANYTHING—LIKE A TENNIS BALL—AND IT WOULD ALL TASTE GOOD.

"That one had to be Alex," I said. "Nobody else has such a twisted mind."

"I take that as a compliment," Alex said proudly.

"Why would anybody want to eat a tennis ball?" asked Olivia, "That's gross!"

"If it tasted good, it wouldn't be gross," Alex explained.

"That's just sick, man," said Logan.

"Hey, we eat pigs and cows and chickens," Alex pointed out. "And did you ever read the ingredients on a box of Twinkies? You might as well eat tennis balls."

"I'm going to assume you were just joking, Alex," Mrs. Walters said as she pulled the next card.

WISH #23:

I WISH I DIDN'T HAVE TO GO TO SCHOOL. SCHOOL IS DUMB.

"Yeah!" said Logan. "That's right. And no books, neither."

"I'll try not to take your wish personally, Logan," said Mrs. Walters.

"It's nothin' against you, Mrs. Walters," Logan said. "But if I didn't have to be here, I could be having fun."

"And what would you be doing if you weren't here?" Mrs. Walters asked.

"Probably out breaking some law," Elizabeth said.

"I would not!" Logan said. "I'd be home playing *Grand Theft Auto*."

"Oh, you wouldn't be breaking the law," Elizabeth said. "You'd *simulate* breaking the law. Much better!"

"That game is not appropriate for kids," said Hannah.

"What do you two know?" Logan asked. "I bet neither of you have ever played the game."

"School isn't dumb," said Natalie. "People who don't go to school are dumb."

"Yeah, if we didn't go to school, we'd be stupid," said Madison.

"Some of us are stupid anyway," Ava said.

"Excuse me," Mrs. Walters interrupted. "But 'stupid' is a word we don't use in this class."

"You just used it," said Logan.

"I know you're all going to make fun of me," Madison said, "but getting a good education is how we grow up to get good jobs, and become good parents and productive members of society."

"Nobody's going to make fun of you, Madison," said Mrs. Walters. "You're absolutely right. I would hate to see what civilization would be like if we didn't have an educational system."

"I didn't say nothin' about anybody *else* going to school," Logan said. "I just wish that *I* didn't have to go."

"I wish you didn't have to go to school either," Abigail said, "because then you wouldn't be here."

Some of the kids laughed. Logan stood up.

"Hey, how come they can say all kinds of mean stuff to me, but I get yelled at whenever I say mean stuff to them? It's not fair."

"You're right, Logan," Mrs. Walters said. "I'm sorry. *Everybody* should be respected. But everyone must go to school too. I'm sorry you don't like it more."

WISH #24:

I WISH I WAS HAPPY ALL THE TIME.

"Don't we all!" said Mrs. Walters.

"I really meant to write *optimistic* more than happy," Mia said.

"So you consider yourself a pessimist?" asked Mrs. Walters.

"Well," Mia said, "I don't like being disappointed. I figure that if I expect that things are going to be bad, and they turn out to be bad, then I'm not so disappointed. And if I expect that things are going to be bad, and they turn out to be good, it's a pleasant surprise. But if I expect that things are going to be good, and they turn out to be bad, it's so depressing. Do you know what I mean?"

"I don't know what the heck she's talking about," said William.

"I know *exactly* what she's talking about," Ethan said. "But that's a messed-up attitude. Why don't you just cheer up? Problem solved."

"It's not as easy as that," Mrs. Walters told Ethan. "If I asked any of you to change your personality and think in a completely different way, it would be very difficult. What if I asked Jacob to stop loving sports, or Isabella to stop loving animals?"

"No way," Isabella said.

"Not gonna happen," said Jacob.

"See what I mean?" Mrs. Walters said.

"You wouldn't want to be happy all the time either," Ella told Mia. "People who are happy all the time are annoying."

"And if you're happy all the time, you're ignoring reality," Natalie said. "If something horrible happened, it would be weird to be happy about it."

"I suppose happiness and sadness should balance each other out," Ella said. "Like two people on a seesaw."

"There's just one more wish," Mrs. Walters said, holding up a card.

I WISH PRINCIPAL HAMILTON WOULD GO SKY-DIVING OVER THE SCHOOL IN HIS UNDERPANTS.

Everybody laughed. Christopher stood up and took a bow.

"You're an idiot," Ethan said. "You know that?"

"It's just a joke," Christopher said.

"It's also the most important decision we'll

ever make," Hannah told Christopher. "I would think you might take it seriously."

"Well, I didn't," Christopher said.

"Okay, that's it," Mrs. Walters announced. "We went through all the wishes. Is there anybody we missed?"

Nobody raised their hand.

"So which one do we choose?" asked Mrs. Walters.

"They're all so different," said Alyssa.

"I can't decide," Anthony said.

"Choose it or lose it," said Bob.

"We need to take a vote," I said. "That's the only fair way."

"There's no time to take a vote!" Ella said. "Look at the clock!"

We all turned to look at the clock on the wall. There was only a minute left. Ella was right. If we started in with a vote, time would run out. We wouldn't get *any* wish, and we'd miss our Christmas vacation.

"You decide, Mrs. Walters," said Ella. "Quick! Just pick something. I'm sure we'll all be happy with whichever wish you choose. We respect your judgment."

"Yeah," we all agreed.

"Well, okay," Mrs. Walters told us. "I would rather have you kids make the decision. But we've got to do what we've got to do. I wish—"

And that's when the bell rang.

PART THREE After

O kay!" Genie Bob said, clapping his little genie hands together. "Time's up! Listen, I'd love to hang around and hear more of your spirited debate and scintillating chitchat, but I really gotta hit the road. Places to go, people to meet. I'm sure ya understand."

"What!?" we all shouted. Everybody was freaking out.

"You can't go *now!*" I shouted at Genie Bob. "We didn't tell you our wish yet."

"Yeah!" everybody else yelled.

"Hey!" Genie Bob said, throwing his hands in the air. "Time's up. You brats blew it. We had a deal. You had an hour. But now the deal is off. The expiration date on me passed. You just lost your Christmas vacation."

"That's not fair!" Logan shouted.

"It's perfectly fair," Genie Bob said. "Deadlines are important in the wishing community. I got my reputation to protect. You had your chance. Wishing for stuff is great and all. But that's only part of the deal. If you wanna see your dreams come true, ya gotta get off your butts and *do* something about it. I'm outta here. *Hasta la vista,* baby! Have a nice life."

Genie Bob closed his eyes and started to float up above the meteorite as he waved good-bye to us. He was about to float right out the window.

That's when William climbed on his desk, jumped up, and dove for Genie Bob. It was the most amazing midair tackle I have ever seen in my life. William tumbled to the floor next to Mrs. Walters's desk, with Genie Bob in his arms. Me and Alex and a few of the other guys piled on too, just to make sure that Bob didn't try to squirm away.

"We want a wish!" William shouted. "You promised us one. And you're not goin' anywhere until we *get* it."

"And we want our Christmas vacation, too!" Alex said.

"Get *off* of me!" Genie Bob shouted.

He was wriggling around trying to break free, but we had him down on the floor pretty good.

"Okay, okay, I usually don't do this," Genie Bob finally said. "I'm gonna make a special exception in your case because you're kids. Even though time is up, I'll grant ya a wish anyway and let ya keep yer vacation, to show ya what a good guy I am. Just get your grubby hands off me. I ain't no football. Sheesh, I bet nobody ever tackled Santa Claus when he was leaving their house."

William let go of Genie Bob, and he floated up to about eye level.

"I wish you *were* Santa Claus, instead of a dumb Christmas genie!" exclaimed William.

Genie Bob stopped.

"What'd you just say?" he asked.

"I said I wish you were Santa Claus," William said.

That's when the most amazing thing in this whole story happened. A smile spread across Genie Bob's face. A twinkle appeared in his eye. Above his upper lip, a mustache began to sprout, and a white beard grew out of his chin before our very eyes.

"No!" shouted Mrs. Walters. "Stop!"

But it was too late. Genie Bob's tie-dyed shirt had already turned a bright red, and white fur trim grew out of it, as if by magic. We stared at him as his pants turned red, held up by a thick black belt and buckle. Red mittens to match appeared on his little hands and a red hat with a white pom-pom at the point grew on his head.

"He's turning himself into Santa Claus!" Logan shouted.

"Wait! No! That's not our wish!" we all started yelling.

But there was no stopping Genie Bob now. His body grew bigger and *bigger* before our eyes until he was the size of a grown man. A grown, extremely fat man.

"Ho! Ho! Ho!" he bellowed as he ran toward the window. "Thanks for making *my* wish come true! Merry Christmas! So long, suckers."

William dove and tried to tackle Genie Bob again, but Bob was much bigger than he was the first time. He straight-armed William like a football player and knocked him down. Genie Bob climbed out the broken window and ran through the playground.

"Ho! Ho! Ho!" he hollered as he disappeared around the corner.

Well, that's pretty much the way it happened. We were all upset that we didn't get a wish, but at least we got our Christmas vacation.

If, by some miracle, I ever get another chance to make a wish, I'm going to think it through a little more. Maybe instead of wishing for a snowboard or a bike or a pile of money for myself, I might wish for world peace or to end global warming or something that might help lots of people. And I figure the Cubs should be able to win without me. We waited a hundred years for them to win the World Series. I guess we can wait a little longer.

Like I said before, you don't have to believe a word of this story if you don't want to. But even if you think I made this whole thing up, it might be a smart idea to come up with a wish or two of your own. Think about your goals and your dreams. Just in case. Because you never know when *your* genie might show up.

But be careful what you wish for. You just might get it.

Check out a preview of Dan's
newest book

The Talent Show

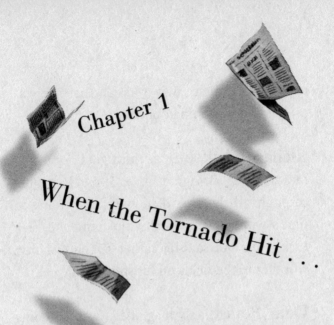

Chapter 1

When the Tornado Hit . . .

- **Paul Crichton**, a fifth grader at Cape Bluff Elementary School in Cape Bluff, Kansas, was alone in his basement with his Fender Stratocaster guitar, trying to master the intro to "Stairway to Heaven."

- **Julia Maguire**, a Cape Bluff fourth grader, was on pointe at The Fontaneau Ballet Studio, rehearsing her relevés and tour jetés for the grand allegro in *Giselle*.

- **Elke Villa**, a sixth grader, was in the shower, belting out "I Will Survive," Gloria Gaynor's

1978 disco anthem, into a loofah that she was pretending was a microphone.

• **Richard Ackoon**, a third-grade aspiring rap star, was sitting on his back porch, paging through his rhyming dictionary, and trying to find a word that rhymed with "humiliate." He looked up and saw his father in the distance, working in the fields on his small farm.

• **Don Potash**, sixth grader, was listening through headphones while watching a stand-up comedy DVD, *Jerry Seinfeld: I'm Telling You for the Last Time*.

• **Lucille Rettino**, the fifty-five-year-old mayor of Cape Bluff, was being photographed with the members of the Cape Bluff Garden Club at their annual fund-raiser.

• **Jon Anderson**, the principal of Cape Bluff Elementary School, was at a desk in his office doing paperwork and sipping coffee.

- **Justin Chanda**, a multimillion-selling pop star who grew up in Cape Bluff, was a thousand miles away at a recording studio in Los Angeles, overdubbing vocals for his next album, *Back to Kansas*.

- **"Honest Dave" Gale** was on the lot of his car dealership, Honest Dave's Hummer Heaven, trying to talk a reluctant customer into buying a Hummer H3T pickup.

- **Mary Marotta**, a stay-at-home mom and proud member of the PTA, was watching *Oprah* while making peanut butter and Marshmallow Fluff sandwiches for her two young children, who had just come home from school.

But *everybody* in Cape Bluff, Kansas, stopped what they were doing when the tornado alarm sounded.

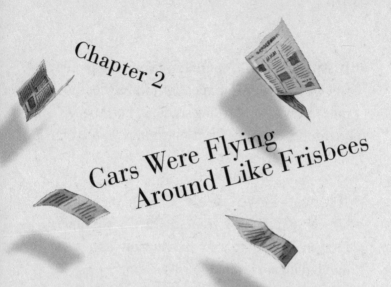

Chapter 2

Cars Were Flying Around Like Frisbees

The animals were the first to realize something was wrong. They always are. At 3:48 p.m. that Tuesday afternoon, the birds in Cape Bluff suddenly stopped singing. Cows huddled close together in the field. Dogs began running around erratically.

Animals have a sixth sense about these things. Maybe it's infrasound—low frequency rumbles that are below the threshold of human hearing.

Anyway, the animals knew before the people. They just knew.

To anyone's eyes in Cape Bluff, at first it looked like a whopper of a thunderstorm was approaching. The cumuliform clouds that dotted the sky all morning had, without anyone noticing, joined into one gigantic darker cloud mass covering the sky and blocking out the sun.

But there was something different this day. The sky took on a sickly yellow/greenish hue. At the local weather station a few miles down the road, a meteorologist jotted down the time in his logbook.

The rains came down for a while, not too heavy. There was even some hail. Then there was an eerie quiet.

Richard Ackoon, the young rapper sitting on his porch, looked up. There had been a sudden change in pressure. The air felt heavy, and hot, like it was too close to his face. He found it hard to breathe.

The enormous cloud was moving fast, and then, suddenly, the wind stopped. It was peaceful. The leaves in the trees tilted up gently, as if they were looking at the sky.

No funnel cloud was visible. Not yet. There was a subtle swirling mist, but nobody could see it. The tube of air was horizontal at first, but gradually the rising air pushed it vertically, until it resembled a spinning top.

Elke Villa, the girl who had been singing in the shower, suddenly stopped when she heard a tornado siren go off in the distance.

Cape Bluff is in the heart of Tornado Alley, a vast area that stretches from parts of Texas to Minnesota. Everyone who lives within that region knows what to do when the tornado siren blares. In school they had tornado drills once a month.

Elke quickly rinsed off and got out of the shower. She threw on a T-shirt and shorts, went into her bedroom, and pulled the mattress off her bed. Then she dragged it into the bathroom. She picked up her dog, Lucky, climbed into the tub, and pulled the mattress over the two of them. She and Lucky would stay there in the bathtub until the all-clear signal sounded.

Mrs. Mary Marotta quickly screwed the cap on the Marshmallow Fluff jar and grabbed the remote control to her TV. She flipped away from *Oprah* and turned to The Weather Channel. The screen was flashing TORNADO WARNING FOR FOUR STATE AREA. But almost instantly the power in her house went out and the screen faded to black. She rushed to get a flashlight and transistor radio from her pantry.

"Mommy, the TV went off!" cried her daughter, Elsie, from the living room. Elsie was in second grade, and her little brother, Edward, was in first.

Mrs. Marotta grabbed each of them by the arm, and hustled them outside to the prefab bomb shelter constructed belowground in the backyard. It had been built in the 1950s, in case of a Russian atomic blast.

When he heard the siren, Paul Crichton, the young guitar god, grabbed his most precious possession—his Strat—and crawled under the workbench in the corner of the basement. That's what his parents had taught him to do. If anything was going to fall on him—like the entire house—he would be protected.

At The Fontaneau Ballet Studio, Julia Maguire and the other students were hustled away from all that glass—the picture window in the front and the giant mirror that covered one whole wall of the studio. The school had no basement. The students were led—in an orderly fashion—into the office and instructed to crouch down in the corner to make as small a target as possible. The leotard-clad girls covered their heads with notebooks, backpacks, or in some cases, just their hands.

All over Cape Bluff, people rushed to prepare for a disaster. Some were hiding in closets, hoping to put as many walls as they could between themselves and the wind. People huddled on the floors of interior rooms, avoiding halls that opened to the outside in any direction. Kids rushed to put on their bike helmets, batting helmets, and hockey masks. Anything to protect themselves from flying objects. Some people crawled into metal trash cans. Parents were exchanging final glances, just in case they would not see one another again.

The storm picked up momentum as it rushed through town. People who were unfortunate enough to be out on the streets of Cape Bluff watched the black funnel approaching, fully aware that a falling tree, power line, or lightning bolt was just as dangerous as the tornado itself.

The smart ones jumped in a nearby ditch and lay there. That's the safest place outdoors, unless of course, you get swept away by a flash flood.

All over town, a continuous rumble could be heard in the distance. As the funnel moved closer, it became a muffled *whoosh*ing sound, like a waterfall or air rushing past an open car window driven at high speed. The roar grew sharper and louder, until it sounded like a freight train or jet engine.

It was officially an F4 tornado. The wind speed topped out at 260 miles per hour. But nobody knew the speed for sure, because at the weather station the device they used to measure wind speed blew away. Trees began to bend, and finally snap.

Some people—some foolish people—ran around their houses frantically opening the windows. They had been told that if the windows are open, it allows a tornado to pass through more easily and cause less destruction.

They were wrong.

The black funnel, now visible for miles, began to stab the earth like a dagger from the clouds. The snakelike tail flipped back and forth underneath it, licking one neighborhood for a minute or two before dancing on to the next one, like a bee trying to decide which flower to pollinate. It lashed out as if it had a purpose, an insatiable twisted mind intent on destroying anything below.

Like a carousel out of control, debris was swirling overhead. Bricks, beams, concrete, chairs, tables, clothes, toys, jewelry, and family heirlooms. Kitchen knives were flung 150 feet per second, impaling anything in their path. Years later, one would be found at a construction site, eight feet below the ground.

At Pete's Lumber Company on the north side of town, two-by-fours were being tossed around like Popsicle sticks. A hundred-year-old oak tree was yanked out by the roots. Cars were flying through the air like Frisbees.

At Cape Bluff Elementary School, the door to the library was ripped off its hinges. Water flooded inside, and virtually every book in the library was ruined.

At Booker's Stamps and Coins, the entire inventory was swept away. In an instant, a lifetime of work that had been so carefully collected and stored was gone.

Objects were plucked off the ground and thrown every which way. A pair of German shepherds was picked up and carried a quarter mile from their home. Miraculously, neither was hurt. An entire maple tree would be found, intact, two miles from where it grew. Forty miles away, a phone bill from a Cape Bluff resident would be found on the street. Debris would be picked up as far as eighty miles away.

Don Potash, the young comedian, had been home alone, watching his portable battery-powered DVD player. He had headphones on and hadn't heard a thing. As he listened to Jerry Seinfeld tell jokes about doing laundry, Don's house began to shudder as if a giant was shaking it. The building vibrated as the roar grew steadily louder. Don was concentrating heavily as he copied down the jokes in his special notebook that was filled with his favorite comedy routines.

By the time Don realized anything was going on, the aluminum siding was being ripped away from the frame of his house like a banana peel. And then, the building literally *exploded* and flew away. Seconds later, you couldn't even tell that a house had ever been on that spot. It had been wiped clean.

All that was left was Don Potash, sitting where his house used to be, dazed and confused, with the headphones still on his head.

And then, after all that . . . nothing. The tornado had done the only thing it knew how to do—destroy things indiscriminately. It suddenly dissipated, exhausted, like a car that had run out of gas.

Just ten minutes after the tornado started, it was all over.

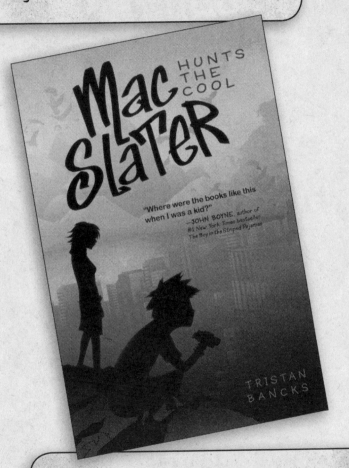

Mac is the coolest kid in town. . . .

He just doesn't know it yet.

Look for *Mac Slater vs. The City* coming Spring 2011!